JOURNEY OF SHADOWs

A fast-paced mystery
where time is the enemy

Chapter One

It should have been easy. A piece of cake, with a few other clichés thrown in. Find a missing person. I felt guilty taking the guy's money, but not for long. Maybe a minute. Five thousand dollars up front, and a hundred and fifty an hour of billed time up to a cool forty grand. Not bad for a private eye who had only been in business for a week. I had trouble looking calm. I almost fell off my rented swivel chair when I heard the deal. But I guess I pulled it off, because I had the check in my hand as he walked out. I had a name and a place to start. I was in heaven.

I was going to give this grand gesture of mine three months. That was when I would have to stop eating, because the money would run out, without a client. I expected to be photographing wandering husbands for pocket change, until maybe a big one walked through the door. As it turned out the big one came first. Funny how things work out. I knew right away that he was money, or at least represented it. He looked like a lawyer, from his buttoned-down shirt to his diamond-studded cuff links. He covered it with a double-breasted suit that looked like silk. His hair was slicked back and glossy, like he had fallen in love with a large bottle of hair spray. I knew he meant business when I looked into his eyes. His stare was fixed on my eyes, waiting for me to react.

"How did you happen to choose me?" As soon as the words left my lips, I regretted saying them. What did it matter why he came through my door, it was a job. I could already taste the porterhouse steak his money would buy, along with a few other things.

"I saw your ad in the phone book, and you were close to my offices. I did some checking and found out you had been in the Marines, with an exemplary service record and a background in intelligence. I thought you could get the job done, and that our money would be well spent". He explained.

'Our money' he said. That proved it. He was working for someone else. I didn't press it. Whoever it was would get their money's worth. I wouldn't pad the expense account either. I might get referrals. That would be worth more in the long run than a few extra bucks I didn't earn.

"When can you start?" he asked.

"My calendar is clear right now. As soon as I have all the information you can give me, I'll be on my way". I thought that calendar thing was cute. I'd just been sitting around waiting for a job since I put up my sign, which wasn't paid for by the way.

"His name is Phillip Atchison. He's third generation, but his namesakes are all deceased, so the three behind his name no longer applies. The last time he was seen was near his home in Richmond, Virginia. The date was October 29th, 1929."

I was stunned. "That was what," I was calculating in my head, "twenty-one years ago and the same day the stock market crashed? It was called Black Tuesday wasn't it?" Then I felt dumb. Everybody knew the significance of that day. "I was only 19, but I remember the panic. Luckily my family was not invested in stocks."

"You were fortunate Mister Dunn." He answered.

"You might as well call me Ivan, since we are going to be associated."

"That's an interesting first name. What nationality is it, if you don't mind my asking?"

"Not at all", I answered. It's Greek. The Dunn part is a shortened American version of a much longer name."

"I see." He was a man of few words.

He knew more about me than I did about him. He'd said his name was Jeremy Taylor.

When he handed me his card the only other piece of information on it was his phone number. He'd said his offices were only a few blocks from here. All that told me was that he worked in Chicago. Oh well I thought, I'll worry about the rest of it if the check doesn't clear.

I was thinking to myself, why wait 'til now to look for this guy? Or perhaps they didn't. It could be that they searched but never found him. Maybe 1950 would be the year.

Before leaving he handed me a rather bulky manila envelope. "This is everything we have on Phillip Atchison. It might help you get started."

"It looks like a lot of information, judging by the weight of it." I said as I lifted it with both hands in a suggestive manner. "I'll have time to look at it on the plane down to Richmond."

"Good luck. I'll be looking forward to your report." were his parting words as he closed the door behind him.

The next day, Tuesday, I went to the bank and deposited the money into my account. Then I waited. My answer came on Wednesday. I had a bonafide client. I called the airport, bought a ticket to Richmond to leave on Thursday, and then celebrated alone with an inch and a half Porterhouse, medium rare.

Jeremy Taylor had been right about his facts. Maybe he knew the whole story, but I didn't think so. I'd been older than most recruits when I joined up early in 1942. I'd already been married and divorced. No kids, luckily. The split came in November of the previous year. Maybe we were doomed from the start, but it took five years to become apparent, at least to Annie. I was still in love, and wanted to continue, but she couldn't take it anymore. We were living in a cheap studio apartment, and behind on our rent. I had become convinced I could make my fortune as a salesman. Unfortunately I was pretty bad at it. I'd also developed a gambling habit. Annie stood it as long as she could and then asked her parents for train fare back to Massachusetts, where they lived. She left on the last day of November, but she took the bus, because I had gambled away part of the money from her parents. A week later the Japanese bombed Pearl Harbor.

It took about a week to make the decision. I was at loose ends, spending all my time in a Chicago bar. I had three bucks and change in my pocket when I walked into the Marine recruiting station. My high school diploma placed me ahead of many of the kids that enlisted that day. They were all full of patriotism, while I just wanted to get away from it all.

Boot camp was tougher than advertised. Most nights I crawled into my bunk and was asleep in minutes. There was no time to think of anything but what the drill sergeant was pounding into our heads. The Corps was everything; your family. You owed your loyalty to only the Corps. I bought it and gave it everything I had.

By the time we were shipped to Camp Pendleton on the West Coast for deployment I had been promoted to Corporal. There wasn't much time to savor that fact, because we were soon crammed into a submarine of all things, and headed out into the Pacific. At first our officers told us nothing. After we were at sea for a couple of days, our skipper, a lieutenant commander named Evans Carlson, laid it out for us. Most of us had never heard of Makin Island.

As it turned out we were sent to wipe out a Japanese garrison, destroy a seaplane base, and boost morale, both in the Corps and at home. The brass also hoped we could divert the enemy's attention from the Solomon Islands where the bigger show was set to begin.

We were able to limit human losses at first by making landfall under cover of darkness, on a night when there was no moon, on a secluded beach. Only a small Jap patrol was encountered and, through surprise, with the use of knives instead of loud gunfire, they were quickly neutralized. After daybreak, however, it was a different story. Remaining undetected was no longer possible. We were able to advance across the island to the seaplane base, but only after repulsing a banzai attack from the Japanese garrison. My sergeant took a round to his chest, and I immediately became a squad leader. We found out later that we had killed most of the occupation force on the island in that futile banzai charge.

I earned my purple heart that day by stopping a bullet with my right leg. I stayed with the main force, but because of my wound, got a priority seat on one of the first rubber boats headed through the surf back to the waiting Nautilus sub. It turned out to be a stroke of luck, because many of the weary jarheads had to remain on the island until the next morning, after trying to breach the increasingly heavy surf and failing. As it was, our boat which had been powered by a small outboard motor, overturned. I was out of it and didn't understand what was happening because of my loss of blood. I was told later that I almost drowned. If it hadn't been for a PFC named Jerry Greenway, who held my head above water as the rest of the crew righted the boat, I could have bought it right there. As it was I guess they had a hell of a time getting me back aboard.

The rest of the journey to the waiting submarine was accomplished with oars. The motor was all that was lost, thankfully. A tourniquet was applied to my leg, and a corpsman aboard the sub stopped the bleeding. We were back at Pearl before I finally woke up. I was transported by PBY to San Diego where I spent the next three months in the Naval Hospital. My knee had been shattered by that bullet and, for me the fighting part of the war was over.

I was reassigned to Intelligence at the Naval Station off Harbor Drive. Even though I had no education or experience in investigative work, I did manage to fit in doing grunt work, chasing down leads, with a heavy emphasis on the paperwork involved with each case. I became a pretty good typist in the process.

When I graduated from crutches to a cane, I decided to give my deteriorated relationship with Annie one more try. She had written a couple of letters that caught up with me when I reached Pearl Harbor. There was nothing in them that even hinted that I had a chance at reconciliation. They could have been written by my sister if I had one. They were very formal and told of things other than love or affection. When the war broke out, she had felt duty-bound, so she came to San Diego and got a job at a defense plant. I could just see her, all one hundred pounds, barely reaching five feet, holding a rivet gun. I wondered at the time if she had cut her long flowing raven colored hair to fit inside her hard hat.

I'd already been in the hospital a month when my first liberty came and went. I was a big man in my thoughts, but when it came time to put up or shut up, I chickened out. I convinced myself she wouldn't be interested in a guy who could hardly walk. Given our history together, and my screw-ups, I knew I needed to be at my best to have a chance with her. By the next weekend my courage had returned. I'd found her name in the phone book. Her address was not too far away, in North Park.

When I boarded a streetcar that Saturday in my pressed dress blue uniform I was pretty nervous. The ride took only twenty minutes, and I had gained back a little courage by then. I found a cottage that matched the address I had, and was surprised. It was pretty nice, but small. There was a garden next to her porch, with mostly flowers. As I walked up the steps leading to her door I saw the doorbell. I pushed it and waited. Nothing happened. No one came. The realization struck me that I should have called first, but the truth was I was afraid she wouldn't want to see me.

The ride back to the base seemed to take longer, but that was probably just in my head. I was disappointed. I really thought we might patch things up. Everything that had led to our split had been resolved, at least in my head. I was a war hero of sorts, with a steady paycheck from the Government. I couldn't get Annie out of my mind. I had this fantasy that when she came to her door to greet me, she wouldn't have any clothes on. It was a good dream.

As fate or the Gods would have it, we did finally meet up. I was still attached to the Naval Hospital. A corpsman and I were at an upscale bar in the El Cortez hotel one evening about three weeks after my sojourn to her rented cottage. I spotted her at a table. She was engaged in an animated conversation with a Navy Lieutenant-Commander who was seated at her table. I boldly walked up to them and said smiling, "Hi stranger. Fancy meeting you here." I hoped she didn't think I was following her.

She was genuinely surprised, and seemed happy to see me. "Ivan! Wow. It's so good to see you. I'd you to meet James Priestley. Jim is attached to a ship here in the harbor."

He stood up and we shook hands. He had a good smile, and I hate to say I liked the guy. "What ship are you on Commander?" I had to be formal. I was in uniform, and so was he. I didn't have to salute, though, because we were indoors.

"I was just assigned to the Sims. It's a destroyer." He answered.

Annie interrupted, "He's the executive officer." She said proudly, as if he was an admiral.

Then I saw the ring on her left hand. It suddenly brought a sense of finality to our relationship. "Look, I just came over to say hello. I'll leave you two to enjoy your evening. Nice to meet you Commander. Good luck with your new ship."

Annie smiled, but didn't say anything. It was an awkward moment for us both.

"You too, Marine. Stay safe." He didn't know that my fighting days were over.

When I was released from the hospital, my orders for Washington, D.C. came through, and I left for the east. It would be years before I returned to Southern California.

Chapter Two

When Jeremy Taylor left Ivan Dunn's shabby office he walked to the next block where a black Rolls Royce limousine was parked. The driver jumped out from behind the wheel and came around to the sidewalk, so as to open the door for his passenger. Neither man said a word as the big car left the city and travelled into the country. Soon they were by a large gate connected to an eight foot wall, that appeared to circle a huge estate. It took another five minutes after the gate opened to arrive at what appeared to be the front door of the main house. Two white pillars, reminiscent of the plantations of the deep-south, guarded both sides of the door, and extended at least four stories to a green gabled roof. "Who needs a house this large?" Jeremy thought to himself while waiting for someone to come let him in. He remembered thinking the same thing when he first sighted the monstrous property two days earlier.

As before, he was led into a large study with dark oak shelves lined with books covering two walls. His guide quickly exited through one of the two doorless openings. He had the feeling his wait would be long, so he placed himself in one of the two large soft chairs that were spaced about eight feet apart, facing one another. It was another ten minutes before anyone appeared.

She wheeled herself into the spacious room from the second of the two entryways. Jeremy found himself wondering if all the openings were made that way in deference to her condition. She was a handsome woman in her late sixties, he assumed. She was dressed immaculately, from her flat functionally tasteful shoes, to an ankle length powder blue fitted dress that showed her slimness. He wondered how she kept trim in her situation. Her dark brown hair was cut fairly short, and she obviously had just had a permanent. The only part of her countenance that didn't seem to fit were her eyes. They were brown, which was okay, but they seemed dull, as if the love of life that had once been there, was now gone. She seemed rather sad.

"I hope your presence here means that your business has been concluded successfully", she opened.

"Very successfully I think", he said using her term.

"Do you think he suspected anything?" She wheeled herself closer to him, intent on his answers.

"No, not at all. The money offer seemed to take all his interest. After he heard how much you were willing to pay for his services, nothing else seemed to matter."

"Good, but you didn't reveal that the request came from me?"

"No. As far as Mister Dunn knows the request came from me, and he is to report to my office." Then as an afterthought, he stated "You were rather extravagant. You probably could have gotten him for half that much, Mrs. Brecker."

"I wanted to be sure he would take the job. Besides, I have more money than I will ever be able to spend, thanks to my late husband."

Jeremy had heard of Paul Brecker. He was an accountant, some say for the mob. There were a lot of stories going around Chicago about how he accumulated his fortune. No one seemed to know for sure, but his worth was estimated to be in the millions. Elizabeth was a widow acquaintance of a friend of Paul's, so the story goes. It was about 1935 when he took a fancy to her. They were married soon after. His wife was not lucky in love, however. He disappeared about the same time in 1945 that FDR died. The country was in panic mode, because of the loss of their beloved President, and the ongoing world war, and little time was spent delving into the accountant's disappearance. No conclusions were ever reached, and his wife was able to have him declared legally dead in 1948, thereby freeing up his sizable estate.

"Tell me about Mr. Dunn. I've never met the man. What does he look like?"

"He's a tall fellow, about six feet I'd guess. He's rather slim, but muscular like an athlete. When I saw him he wore no jacket, with a white collared shirt and no tie. His gabardine slacks looked as if they needed to be pressed."

"But what about his features? I would like to be able to recognize the man if I ever have occasion to meet him." She looked away as if disinterested.

"His hair is very dark, and wavy, but not too long. His chin was narrow, and jutted out slightly- rather Lincolnesque, if you ask me. He has a thin mustache. I think he would stand out in a small crowd, but not a large one." He laughed.

She ignored his attempt at humor. "Do you think he's competent enough to have success in finding Phillip Atchison?" She jolted him back to reality.

"It's hard to say. He didn't ask the hard questions that would have led him in the right direction. The money shocked him, I'm sure. If it were me I would have looked for someone with more experience. But that didn't seem to be an option with you." He looked at her, hoping he hadn't overstepped his bounds.

"Careful, Mr. Taylor. Remember you are just an employee. My reasons shouldn't interest you."

"Sorry. Curiosity apparently can get me in trouble." He hoped he'd smoothed it over.

She laughed. "You did your job well. I am thankful for your professionalism, even though it's contrived."

"I am rather good you know. I suppose I must give back the wardrobe?" It was a question. He'd grown rather fond of looking successful.

"No you keep it, as a memento of a job well done. Did you give the detective the phone number to report in?"

"Yes. It's on the card with my name. I'm assuming it connects to this address?"

"You assume correctly. Your secretary will answer it when needed." Elizabeth answered. "It seems that our business is concluded Mr. Taylor. Thank you for a job well done." With that obvious dismissal, she wheeled her chair around and left the room the way she had come.

Chapter Three

When I boarded the twin-engine Lockheed Electra for the flight to Richmond I was nursing a massive headache. I found myself wishing through the pain that I hadn't celebrated quite so much. At least I remembered to bring the manila envelope that, hopefully, would give me a place to start the search for Phillip Atchison. The two and a half hour flight should give me enough time to sort out my thoughts and develop a plan of action, if I could work around the buzz in my head.

I opened the bulky envelope, tipping it upside down over the tray table in my lap. The first thing I noticed was the picture. It was of a teen-aged boy, mounted on a painted stallion, and dressed as a cowboy, with chaps, a ten-gallon hat, and a holster with twin pistols hanging out. I thought that was a little strange. Teens, even in the twenties, were more interested in flappers than cowboy stuff. They were more likely to dress up as prohibition mobsters, with shoulder holsters and derbies-or cops. Oh well, I thought, "To each his own."

Next I picked up a map of the Richmond area. I guessed that could be helpful. My thoughts were interrupted when the stewardess brought me a glass of bromo-seltzer, foaming nearly to the brim. I thanked her and downed it quickly. It was bitter-tasting stuff, but I deserved to suffer. The pretty young lady was still standing there, so I handed her the now empty glass and thanked her again. I watched her as she walked away, and wished I had struck up a conversation. Maybe later. She looked like she would be worth it. Of course they all did. They came out of the same mold, mostly blonde, with a brunette thrown in once in a while. They had twenty-three inch waists, and they apparently didn't fall over wearing four-inch heels.

I was letting myself become distracted. Back to the work at hand. The next item that caught my eye seemed to be a list of names, about ten of them. There were no Atchisons listed. I guess I was supposed to know about them. I tried to remember my conversation with Jeremy Taylor. I couldn't recall that he had said anything about family. I scolded myself silently for being less than attentive. The last name on the list was Rachel Embree. It was separated by a line, as if it were added as an afterthought. Other names that caught my eye were Louise Lambright, and Rodney Lambright. Brother and sister maybe? A school made the list, and a bank, The First Richmond. There was an address, which I assumed was where the family made their home. I made a mental note to start there.

The last thing I saw was the front page of a newspaper. It was dated October 30th, 1929. The headlines were all about the crash, and its immediate aftermath. On page two when I turned it over was the article that changed everything!

When the plane landed I reluctantly said goodbye to twenty-three inch waist, and made my way to the baggage counter. I picked up my one suitcase and headed for the taxi stand outside the terminal. The driver, a displaced New Yorker, recommended a small but tasteful hotel downtown, and dutifully deposited me there after supplying me with a huge dose of political savvy. After talking to him I was surprised the Republic survived.

I was able to obtain a room on the fourth floor overlooking the parking lot. That would come in handy if and when I obtained a car. I could keep an eye on it.

Since it was still reasonably early in the day, I figured to make my first stop at the local newspaper office. I thought that maybe my private detective's license might buy me some first-hand knowledge of what happened so long ago. That is if I could find a reporter old enough to have been working that fateful day.

I realized I wouldn't need a car just yet. The place I wanted was just around the corner from my hotel. When I walked in I knew I was in trouble. There were about ten faces within my view, and none of them looked to be over thirty. One, I assumed to be a reporter, dutifully came to the counter to presumably help me. He looked to be on the low side of twenty. I remember wondering at the time how he became a reporter so quickly.

"May I help you sir?" he asked, in what seemed to me to be a mid-western voice like you might hear on the radio.

I handed him my credentials, and began to speak. He interrupted with "Chicaago, woowie" in a now strictly southern drawl. "y'all are a long way from home, ain't ya." It was not a question.

I looked around the office. All the young faces had stopped what they were doing, and were now intent on what was going on at the counter. I decided that my first instinct was correct. I should have tried the library. But I gave it one more shot.

"I'm looking for old copies of your newspaper."

"And which ones would that be?" the rude youngster asked.

"October 30th, 1929", I said, as matter-of-factly as I could, and waited for a reaction. There was none, except that now everyone had returned to their duties at hand.

"Just you wait here, and I'll see what I can find", the mid-western voice had returned. I guess the war between the states was over after all.

Presently he returned with a stack of slightly brown papers. "I brought you the whole week beginning with the thirtieth, if that's okay." He was suddenly very helpful.

"Great, thank you."

"There's a desk over there in the corner that might be more comfortable. At least you can sit down."

I thanked him again, went to the desk, and found the first paper I needed. It was the same one that Jeremy Taylor had given me in my office in Chicago. It read:

Bank Shooting Investigation Under Way

Prominent banker and civic leader Phillip Atchison II was found dead yesterday in his bank. Another man, identified as John Lambright of Richmond was also shot. No connection between the two men has been established, except that Mister Lambright might have been a bank customer who just happened to be in the wrong place at the wrong time. No weapon has been found, and apparently nothing was taken from the bank.

It seemed strange to me that no gun was found. If it was a murder-suicide the piece would have been right there by Lambright. Either someone else was in the bank and took the weapon after the fact, or that other person committed the murders. And what happened to the other patrons and employees of the bank? Maybe the answer was in later issues of the newspaper. I was looking for some mention of the missing boy too. So far there was nothing.

I was all the way up to November second before I found it. There was just a small item on page three-not even a story really. All it said was that a teen was missing, and presumed kidnapped, but that no ransom had yet been demanded. The boy, Phillip Atchison the third, had last been seen leaving his home last Tuesday the twenty-ninth, the same day his father was murdered. No connection had been established.

There had to be more information available than what I had seen so far. Who saw Phillip leave the house? What time was it? Surely there was school that day. Did he leave early? Then I remembered the list Jeremy Taylor had provided me. He obviously knew about the murder. Why didn't he mention it? It wasn't just a small thing. The name Lambright was in my head for some reason. It was on the list. That's right. A man and woman had the same last name, and sure, it was the same name as the other man killed in the bank that day. There had to be a connection there.

I gathered up the newspapers I had spread on the desk, and took them back to the counter. Right away the same employee came up to the other side and said "Did you find what you were looking for, Mister Chicago?"

I smiled and answered "Some of it. I wonder if I could trouble you for a local phone book." I thought that at this point a little courtesy might be better than the sarcasm I really felt.

"You betcha." He had slipped into the drawl again. This was quite a character. If he can help what does it matter if he's having fun with me?

When he brought the book I looked for the name Lambright. There were three. None matched the first names I was looking for. I had better luck with the police station. I quickly wrote the address of the precinct closest to downtown, along with the phone number. Then I returned the book to the counter, yelled thank you to anyone within earshot as I walked out the door leading to the street.

Chapter Four

I had a lot to think about as I headed back on foot to the hotel. I had the feeling that if I figured out what really happened in that bank I'd be closer to knowing the answer to why Philip Atchison the third disappeared, and where he went. I didn't buy the kidnapping theory, mainly because, with the stock market collapse, I doubted that his family had any money left to obtain their son's freedom. That didn't rule out the possibility that they might have had enemies who wanted to hurt them in some way, and that could explain senior's demise in the bank. Nothing was missing at the scene, according to the news reports I read, and that could support the revenge theory. Was the Lambright fellow just an unlucky bystander, or did he play a role in the whole thing? Not the least puzzling was what happened to all the customers and bank employees during the time of the killings? It was just after noon according to the accounts I read. The place should have been thriving with activity, especially given the events that were occurring on Wall Street.

Once in my room I laid out the notes I'd taken at the newspaper office on the small coffee table in front of a sofa that had seen better days. It sagged in the middle and was frayed around the edges. Oh well, I thought, the price was right.

Maybe a part of the answer was in a timeline of that day's events. I decided to write it out chronologically. I had just started when there was a knock on the door.

Through force of habit I looked in that little thing that's supposed to give you a view of the person or persons that have intruded on your privacy. All I saw was the top of a man's head. Since nobody knew me in this town and couldn't possibly hold a grudge, I opened the door. A very short man, maybe five foot four, stood there. I'd never seen him before. "Yes", I said eloquently.

"Are you that detective that was in the newspaper office?" He said in a rather intimidating voice.

"Who wants to know?" I could play that game too. Why should I be afraid of a little man with a bald head. My answer came when I looked farther down and saw the gun in his hand.

I changed my tone to fit the situation. Before the little man could answer I said, "Yes, my name is Ivan Dunn, and who might you be?"

"Who I am doesn't matter. Why are you digging into old news?"

I looked at him. He wasn't the menacing type. He looked to be about the same age as me, about forty. He wore a suit. His shoes were shined. It just didn't fit. "I was hired to find somebody" I answered. I thought about rushing him, but that was a big gun.

"What somebody?" He waited.

"A kid who went missing a long time ago. He was living here at the time." I didn't see any reason to hide information at this point.

"Then it has to be Phillip Atchison, doesn't it?"

"That's right." I decided to press forward. "Do you know anything about his disappearance?"

"Never mind that!" He sounded menacing again. It still didn't match up. "Why were you looking in the old papers?"

"I was trying to find a clue to what happened to the kid, that's all." This line of questioning didn't make any sense to me. Why the gun? That didn't compute either. I would have told him the same things without it.

"Did you find anything that would help?" He questioned with a growl.

"Not much. I don't even know if he was gone before his old man got shot, or after. There doesn't seem to be any clear connection."

Suddenly my assailant backed toward the door, and without a word he was gone. I thought about what had just happened. I'd like to meet the little runt without the equalizer. Then I would find out just what he knows, and I wouldn't be the one answering the questions.

I went back to the coffee table, and looked at what I'd accumulated so far. It wasn't much. I decided to go to the local police as my next step. After that it would be back to the list Jeremy Taylor had provided. I would check out each name, if they were still in town. Maybe I'd get lucky and the whole damn mystery would unravel. I doubted it though. Luck had a way of eluding me.

Chapter Five

I slept in on Friday, not waking up until I heard the maids outside my door. I looked at the clock by my bedside. It was 9:30. By the time I had showered and dressed, it was almost noon. So I had lunch for breakfast at a café a few blocks west of the hotel. It was on the way to my first stop of the day-the local police station.

The uniformed cop at the front desk appeared to be a sergeant, if that's what three chevrons meant. When he finally looked up from the papers in front of him he studied me before speaking.

"Yes?" His tone of voice gave me the impression that he thought I had interrupted something important

. I showed him my detective's papers, and as he appeared to read them, I said, "I've been hired to find one of your citizens, a Phillip Atchison. He disappeared a long time ago. I was hoping that maybe someone in your precinct could fill me in on a few details."

A uniformed policeman, nearby, who was also a sergeant, overheard what I had said and walked up to me. He was older than the one at the desk. "I worked that case, Black Tuesday wasn't it?"

"Yes. I hope you have a good memory. I could use the help filling in a few holes."

"It was strange. There were no leads. Nobody saw the kid after he left his home that day. We waited, but there was no ransom note. It was as if he fell off the edge of the earth."

I was surprised by his cooperation. I knew that police and private detectives seemed to be on opposite sides of the fence, and the cops had the power. That left us out in the cold usually. But this guy seemed eager to share what he knew. Maybe it was because he was older. I put him at around sixty.

"And you found no connection to the bank murder?"

"No. But in my gut I think they have to be related. It was just too much of a coincidence."

"What about the murder weapon? According to news reports it was never found?." I queried.

"That was really strange. We did find the piece a few days later. It was in a boxcar of a freight train parked on a side-rail in Wheeling, West Virginia. That's what made us think it was a transient who did the deed for a quick payday."

"But no money was missing was it? Wouldn't whoever it was clean the place out if he went to so much trouble to kill two people?"

"We think he got spooked after the killings, and just needed to get away." The agreeable cop answered.

"I guess that sounds plausible, but you'd think the temptation of all that cash would outweigh his common sense." I still didn't buy the theory. "How many bullets were fired from the gun you recovered?" I asked as an afterthought?

"The FBI said four cartridges were spent."

"Wait a minute. How did the FBI become involved". I was really curious about that, but felt foolish when the uniformed policeman answered.

The cop didn't hesitate, "It was a suspected kidnapping. They were automatically called in, and to be truthful, we needed the help. Then when the weapon turned up it appeared that the killer or killers had crossed state lines in their escape."

I had a thought. "What about fingerprints?"

"There was nothing useable in the bank. All we found were smudges and prints of the people you would have expected to be in there at one time or another."

"How about the gun? Did you get anything from that?" I was pretty sure I knew that answer, with my luck.

"No. It had been wiped clean."

Well that did it. There was nothing more to go on. I thanked the helpful public servant, got his name, which was Andrew Dark, and walked out into a pouring rain, thankful that it was summer. At least it wasn't cold.

Since I didn't have an address for either of the Lambrights on the list, I decided to find the woman Rachel Embree if I could. I located a phone booth nearby, and looked up her name. I found it rather quickly. I wondered at the time if it was her married name, and I might have to deal with a husband.

At this point I decided to rent a car after all. I walked back to the Richmond Gazette office to see if I could get directions to the airport, where the car rentals should be. The same brash young kid was the first one to see me. He had a surprised look on his face as he spoke:

"I didn't expect to see you again."

"Why not, you were so helpful the first time?" I questioned facetiously.

"I thought you would have solved the mystery by now, that's all." He seemed oblivious of my sarcasm.

"No, maybe a few more hours." Before he could retort, I continued, "Could you point me in the right direction to get a bus to the airport? I need to rent a car."

He surprised me be saying, "I can do better than that, Mister Chicago detective. I'm done for the day. I'll take you there."

I would have fallen off my stool, if I'd been sitting on one. This was a complete turnaround. "That would really help. Thank You."

There was very little conversation during the twenty minute ride. The now helpful newspaper guy dropped me off in front of the arrival gate at the Richmond airport, with nothing more than a "good luck". Then he drove off.

I had no trouble at the Hertz counter. They even gave me a map, and pointed me in the right direction. Twenty minutes later I was in front of a little cottage on the east edge of town.

As I walked up to the door of the porch-less house, I noticed the name Embree on the mailbox next to the screen door. There was no buzzer, so I knocked a little more loudly than I had intended. Soon the door behind the screen opened and a rather handsome woman I assumed to be in her late thirties appeared.

"Yes, may I help you?" She said in a rather husky, pleasant voice.

"Are you Mrs. Rachel Embree?" I asked, in my nicest manner.

She corrected me, "Miss. And you are?"

"Hi. I'm Ivan Dunn. I'm looking for Phillip Atchison." I decided to take a direct approach. Right away I saw that it was the wrong course of action. Her knees buckled and she fell to the floor behind the screen. I could do nothing to stop or protect her because I was on the other side of the barrier. I quickly opened the screen door, which luckily was unlatched, bent down and picked her head up from the cold linoleum, sat down, and cradled her in my lap. Her eyes were shut. I looked at her, thinking that she was rather beautiful after all, not just handsome. Maybe it was her helplessness that struck me.

Just then she woke up, looking into my eyes. She was even prettier with her eyes open. Her brown pupils went well with her slightly tanned skin. "What happened?" she said, quickly standing up. There was a look of fear in her eyes. She was tall for a female, standing nearly six feet. With heels I doubt that I could see over her head. All her parts were in exactly the right place for my money. Her breasts were full, but not over-large for her weight, which I guessed to be about one forty.

"You fainted. You hit the floor pretty hard. Are you all right?"

Her hands went to her body near her waist, which I also approved of, as if to inspect for damage. "I appear to be in one piece, thank you. She was looking at me with an unasked question on her lips.

"I couldn't catch you because of the screen. I'm sorry." I meant it. She could have really hurt herself.

"Why are you looking for Phillip? Has there been a development?" Now there was a hopeful look on her face.

"No. I was hired to find out what happened to him. That's why I came to you. I have a list of people to contact, and you're on it. I'm not sure why." I was being honest.

"What is your name again?" she asked.

"My name is Ivan, I'm a private detective from Chicago. A man named Jeremy Taylor hired me to find Phillip. He didn't tell me about the murder at the bank. At this point I'm really confused. Will you tell me what part you have in all this?" I asked plaintively.

She looked around, as if suddenly realizing we were still standing in her doorway. "Please come into the living room, Mr. Dunn, and I'll tell you what I know."

When we were both seated comfortably, she said, "Phillip and I were in love. Nobody knew about it though. His family was really high up in the social standings in Richmond, and I lived across the railroad tracks, if you know what I mean."

"I'm afraid I do." I responded. "Please continue."

"We were both seventeen, and in our final year of high school. Phillip was being groomed to work in his father's bank. He went along with his family's plans, and he was not unhappy, but he wanted to be a writer. They wanted to send him off to an ivy-league college in the fall of 1930. We planned to be married and go to the northeast together. Once there he could study journalism. His family didn't know about me. They thought he was going out with Louise Ormsby. She was a debutante, and a very desirable partner for an aspiring banker. The girl was a clinging vine type, and very possessive. Phillip went out with her for appearances sake, but he loved me." She paused to catch her breath.

"I'm surprised you could keep your feelings secret." I interjected.

"It wasn't easy," she replied. "We could only meet once a week, except at school, where we had to be careful."

"So what happened on the day he disappeared?" I leaned forward in my chair, intent on the next part of her story, not knowing if she would be able to shed any light on the mystery of Phillip Atchison's disappearance, "Did you see him on that last day?"

Rachel looked thoughtful, peering up at the ceiling. I knew she was trying to decide if she could trust me. Hell, I was a complete stranger to her. I couldn't blame her. I would not have told me anything. I decided to ease the sudden tension that had invaded the small living room. I asked her for a drink of water.

It was as if the heavy weight she was carrying had fallen away. She smiled and said "Of course. It was thoughtless of me not to offer you something to drink."

She walked to the adjacent kitchen, found a glass in her cupboard and filled it with tap water. When she returned and handed me the glass, she obviously had made up her mind. She looked me square in the eyes and said "He came to my house right after it happened. He told me everything!"

Chapter Six

It was just an average day in Richmond for October. The sweet smell of Magnolia blossoms was in the air, in advance of an impending fall storm, the first of the season. The clouds that would sweep in had not yet appeared on the horizon, and there was only a fresh breeze. There was not a hint of the distress to come. No one could have known that the nearly idyllic life they had shared would be shattered and gone forever, and that each of their destinies would be altered in ways they could not even imagine.

When Phillip awoke that morning he was nervous. He had slept fitfully off and on all night in anticipation of the confrontation that was to come. But he had to get it over with. School was scheduled to end at noon due to a teacher's conference. This might be the perfect opportunity to break the news to his father. The old man would be at work, but being the bank president and owner should give him leeway to talk to his son. The boy had already broached the subject with his mother. She'd been sympathetic in a cautious manner.

They both knew the man of the house would be the toughest sell.

His father had determined just the day before that once Phillip's studies were over and he graduated, he would begin Summer apprenticeship at the bank. It would give him a head start, a leg up so to speak, so that a career would be assured in a profession that would allow him to access the same luxuries his mother and father enjoyed.

Phillip Atchison the third had it made. He would gain the tools in the banking business to become even more successful than his father, and his namesake too, for that matter. Grandfather Phillip, to his credit, had been hindered slightly by that inconvenient War between the States, and reconstruction, but in the end he had outsmarted those fancy, swindling thieves from the north, and made a bundle doing it. It didn't matter that what he did was slightly, if not downright fraudulent. Phillip was never told what it was his grandfather did for a living, just that he was damn good at it. All his money was dutifully passed down to his heirs upon his demise, which came abruptly on the same day the twentieth century was ushered in.

Phillip wanted to be a writer, like his idol John Faulkner, or at least a journalist for a large newspaper. He knew it would be hard.

Not at all like the banking career that his father had envisioned for him. He had to make his elder understand. He could put off the confrontation and endure more sleepless or restless nights. He didn't want to do that. This time he had to stand up to the man. Just going along was no longer an option.

Going along was what Phillip was good at. When his father told him to do something, he never questioned it. Like when he wanted to play baseball for his school. He had played some sandlot ball, and was fairly good. He had a strong arm and was not afraid of the hard ball. That made him a good choice for third-baseman. In his junior year, as luck would have it, the regular hot corner player had graduated, leaving an opening for Phillip. When he told his father about his good fortune, Two, as the older man was affectionately referred to, did not yell and scream at his son. Instead he reasoned with the boy that he would be needed at the bank from time to time, and the timing was unfortunate. He would be able to earn money for the summer. That would allow him to take Louise Ormsby to dinner or a movie, maybe even both.

Phillip was interested in money, but not for the reason his father expected. Sure Louise was good looking, and she was certainly interested in him, but she was a snob. She was a socialite, if you could call a teenager that. Her family had money, and lavishly endowed their only child with it. She looked down on anyone less fortunate than her.

She despised Rachel Embree, and for good reason in her mind. Rachel was much prettier, and Phillip was obviously attracted to her. But the unforgiveable trait the other girl had was that she was poor. In Louise's mind she just didn't fit in.

Louise Ormsby fancied herself a dancer. She fantasized that she would someday grace a Broadway stage. Of course she would be a rich performer, for she wouldn't give up the family money. She didn't consider that most successful dancers were tall, and she was barely five-foot three. That was another thing she resented Rachel for. The five-foot ten statuesque girl from the undesirable side of town towered over her.

Phillip was definitely smitten with the dark-haired girl from across the tracks. He kept that fact hidden from his parents. His father would never approve, and his mother always went along with her husband. She would never call him Two, but acquiesced to all his other wishes, which sounded strangely like commands.

When the school bell sounded just before noon, Phillip headed directly for the exit door. He had a little more than a mile walk ahead of him to reach the bank, and his sure confrontation with his father.

The Richmond State Bank was situated on the closest side of the downtown section of the city to the school. Only residential houses sat along the route that Phillip used to reach his destination. On the weekend the streets would be thriving with activity-children in the street playing games, and parents bustling around to and fro heading into town to do shopping, or returning with groceries and the like. But on a Tuesday the streets were deserted. Phillip beat all the other children out of school, so the ones that travelled home in that direction were still blocks behind.

As he rushed to meet his father, Phillip had no idea of the chaos that was developing in the financial sector of Richmond and all the other cities across the nation. He was anxious, but not for the reason everyone else was.

The stock market had been on a roller-coaster ride lately, but the public perception was that the worst was over, and it was once again safe to invest. Up until recently, putting savings into stocks had allowed the average investor to realize a much bigger gain than what banks could offer. Some bankers loaned money to investors who couldn't cover the costs of the securities, but didn't want to miss out on the huge profits. It was coined "buying on margin". Phillip Two had jumped at the chance to earn a huge amount of interest from these loans. Sure there was a risk, as average people who couldn't really afford to gamble on the Market, jumped in without thinking of the consequences if the stocks fell. But the banker also felt the excitement that comes when easy money is to be made.

By ten AM on the morning of October 29th it had become apparent to TWO that financial institutions were in the grip of what could turn out to be a general panic. He made a decision to close the bank, after calling all the investors with outstanding debt, informing them that he was instituting a "Margin call"-thereby cancelling all their stock loans, and requiring immediate payment. He sent all his employees home for the day, and locked his doors. It was the first time in all the years he had been in business that the extreme measure was necessary.

John Lambright received a call from Phillip Atchison the second around eleven that morning. He was devastated. Everything had seemed fine a couple of days ago. He had seen the banker at their club, and talked with him briefly. They'd been concerned about the market earlier, as stocks tumbled, but now Wall Street was on the rebound. Everyone felt it was just a temporary pause in the steady climb that would make them all richer.

It hadn't seemed like a gamble in July when Lambright had sunk all the family's discretionary money into stocks, or in September when he signed the papers at the bank for the loan. He was positioned to make a killing that would give his family financial security for life.

Before he started wagering on the market John considered himself a reasonable family man. He spent much of his time at home, doting over his son who was an only child. He and his wife had a loving relationship, which was readily apparent to all who saw them together. Their son Rodney was a precocious teenager, finding mischief, and embroiling himself in it whenever possible. John used a gentle hand to discipline his child, thinking all the time that the coming years would temper the boy's enthusiasm for trouble.

A small manufacturing company occupied much of Lambright's time. He made light bulbs, which were in great demand. What time that was left, after the family he adored, was spent collecting weaponry, a hobby he began after the Great War. He was able to pick up several rifles and pistols from returning servicemen. They were mostly German, though a few of Italian make were available too. By 1929 at the age of forty-five he was the owner of fourteen guns. Most were in working order. He built a case to hold them all, and proudly displayed the collection in his living room.

John felt betrayed by the banker he thought to be his friend. Why had he not received better advice from the professional. Perhaps he could persuade TWO to rescind the margin call, thereby saving him from ruin. He was sure the stock market would rebound, given enough time.

He had ammunition for only three of the guns in his case, one of which was a German Luger. It was his favorite of the lot. On this day he removed it from its perch, thinking it might make a fine exclamation point to his argument. He had no intention of using the weapon, though absently he loaded it.

This work day was unusually quiet at the bank, with the door locked and no customers. After TWO had made all his phone calls he remembered that his son was coming by after school let out. It pleased him that Phillip seemed to be taking an interest in the bank. The boy had seemed distracted the past few weeks. In fact, ever since question of playing baseball came up, there was very little give and take between them at all. Maybe he was still disappointed. Well, time would take care of that, he thought.

As the clock struck noon, the banker moved to the door of the bank and unlocked it. He went outside briefly to see if his son was in view, then not seeing him he went back to his office, which was around twenty feet to the left of the door. He would have unlocked the back entrance to the business, but his son would surely approach on the main thoroughfare.

It was exactly noon when John Lambright, the pistol in his inside coat pocket, left his house for the ten minute drive to his destination.

Chapter Seven

There was no traffic on the end of town where the bank was situated so Lambright was able to find a parking place right in front of his destination. It was not unusual to find the door unlocked at midday, so he gave it no thought.

When he walked in, Phillip Atchison the second came out of his office, expecting to see his son. Surprise showed on his face as he said, "John, it's good to see you. Won't you step into my office?"

Suddenly a look of anger appeared on Lambright's face. How dare him trying to be pleasant after what he did, he thought, as he took a step closer to his so-called friend.

"Please come and sit down. Can I get you some coffee?" The banker said, as he turned to return to his office. The customer's next words stopped him in his tracks however.

"How could you treat me this way, as long as we have known each other, and I've been a customer of this bank. I need you to retract your loan cancellation!"

TWO turned back to his customer. "I can't do that John. I'm not treating you any differently than my other outstanding loans. The bank won't survive with all this debt on the books."

Lambright would have none of this, even though it sounded reasonable. "Look Atchison, you don't understand. My family will face ruination unless you reinstate my obligation."

At this point in the conversation, Phillip Atchison the second made a critical mistake. He laughed. It was a nervous giggle actually, because of the futility of the situation.

Lambright snapped. He pulled out his pistol, aiming it at the helpless banker.

Just then the front door opened, and young Phillip entered. Almost simultaneously the sound of the shell exploding from the gun in John Lambright's hand filled the bank.

"NO!" screamed the boy as he saw his father crumple to the floor.

Before Lambright could turn the gun in Phillip's direction, the boy grabbed him, at the same time trying to pull the weapon away. Somehow the barrel turned upward just as Lambright's finger once again squeezed the trigger.

The projectile went into the ceiling above the two combatants, but not before travelling through the head of a now dead John Lambright.

Phillip stepped back quickly, letting go of his adversary as he did. The man's now limp body fell to the floor with a thud as if he were a sack of potatoes. The boy began shaking uncontrollably as he looked toward where his father lay, unmoving. His mind was racing, unable to grasp fully what had just happened. 'Who was this murderer who lay at his feet? Why did this happen? Was it all a dream? Yes that was it. He would wake up any second.'

A few moments later that seemed like much longer, Phillip, his mind clear now and realizing that it wasn't just a nightmare, at least the kind you sleep through, moved quickly to where his father lay motionless.

The man's eyes were open but there wasn't a flicker of recognition. His chest was still, with a widening red stain in the middle of his dress shirt. Phillip tried to raise a pulse, but there was none. He began to cry, wiping at the tears as soon as they appeared on his red cheeks.

He looked toward the entrance of the bank. No one had appeared. Maybe the sound of the two gunshots went unheard outside. Suddenly he realized how this scene would look to an outsider, to the police. He was the only one left alive. Surely it would appear as if he had killed both men. No one had been around when he entered the bank. He was sure that, up to that point, he had been unnoticed.

He hadn't realized before, but the German Luger used in the killings was in his right hand. He must have wrested the gun from the dead intruder as he fell. He stuck it in his waistband and pulled his shirt out to hide it.

The back door of the bank opened onto an alley. Phillip had used it many times to visit his father. He looked around one more time. Nothing had changed. The two bodies were exactly where they had fallen. There was blood on the ceiling above the corpse of the man he had wrestled with. When he exited he had no idea where he would go, or what he would do. He just knew that he was now a fugitive, and nothing would ever be the same.

Chapter Eight

"So I'm assuming he wasn't seen leaving the bank, since none of the accounts I read mentioned him in association with the bank murders", I said.

Rachel, coming back from her kitchen with a couple of lemonades, looked at me quizzically. "Oh, didn't I mention that?" Then, before I could answer, she continued, "No, he was not detected at all."

"How did you find out what happened? Did he come here to see you, or did he send a letter?" I was hoping it was the latter, since it might have a postmark that would lead me to him.

"He came here."

I was disappointed. Nothing comes easy, except talking to this woman. There was something about her that just made me feel at home. She wasn't hard to look at either. I liked that she was tall. Her dark brown hair was cut short, not at all like most of the women of her day. It had an upward curl that kept it off her neck. She was dressed tastefully in a light skirt that fell to just below her knees, revealing slim legs and ankles that were tanned from the sun. But what really got to me were her eyes. Her pupils were the same color as her hair. She seemed to have no makeup on, which was fine by me. She didn't need any. Her eyebrows were thin, but dark.

She was speaking again. "He had his school clothes on. I gave him a pair of pants and a shirt that belonged to my father. They were a little baggy, but better than the knickers he had on."

I could picture that. He would have stood out wearing the boyish clothes. "Did he say where he was going?" I held my breath waiting for her to speak.

Rachel didn't answer right away. It was obvious she was fighting with herself again whether to trust me or not. When she finally spoke, she had a pained look on her face.

"All he told me was that he had an uncle in Texas. I can't remember the town. It was one I'd never heard of. He said it was in the northeast corner of the state. He also said he'd write when he got there, but he never did."

"So when he left you that day, you never heard from him again?"

"That's right. I thought we were in love, but I guess I was fooling myself. I waited a long time to hear something, just a sign that he was all right. But nothing ever came." Now she looked sad.

'Poor kid', I thought. It sounds like it was more than just young love, at least to her. Then I had another thought. "What happened to his mother? She's not on my list. Is she still in Richmond?"

"No. As I remember, she left town right after her husband's funeral. I never heard anything about her after that." She said, thoughtfully.

"That had to be one hell of a blow, losing your husband and your son on the same day." I said, looking out the window at the waning light of day. "I can't believe how quickly the time went. You've put up with me for quite a while."

"Oh I didn't mind, after the initial shock that is." She answered.

"I'm sorry about that. Next time I'll be more tactful." Silently I hoped there would be a next time. She was nice to talk to.

When we reached her front door, she held out her hand. I shook it, and held on a little longer than I should have. It made for an awkward moment. She blushed as I said, "I guess I don't really want to go. You've been really pleasant, and very helpful."   That seemed to smooth it over, and she smiled as she opened the door.

As I started for my car, she took a step outside. Then I heard it. It sounded like a car backfiring, but there were no other vehicles around. Suddenly she uttered "Oh," and fell backward toward the door of her house, clutching her chest just below her left shoulder.

I realized then that she'd been shot. I fell on top of her instinctively, trying to protect her. Whoever was shooting at me had just missed. I didn't want it to happen again.

It became very quiet. She had fallen over backwards. I looked at her face. Her eyes were closed, but I could tell she was breathing as our bodies moved up and down slowly. I rolled off her and crawled to where her screen door was. I reached up and opened it. Reaching back, I grabbed Rachel's right arm and pulled her slowly toward me. It had been a couple of minutes since the shot, so I took a chance and stood up, still holding onto her arm. I pulled the still woman back into the house and closed the door behind us.

I found her phone on the wall, dialed zero, and waited. The operator came on the line in what seemed to be about five minutes, but was in actuality only about thirty seconds. I yelled into the receiver "This is an emergency. Give me the police!

The female voice on the other end of the line acted quickly this time. A man's voice answered right away, "This is the police. What is your emergency?"

"A woman has been shot!" I blurted out nervously. I quickly gave him the address I had written down earlier. "The gunman may still be outside, and I don't have a weapon."

"Lock yourselves in as best you can, and stay away from the windows. A squad car and ambulance are on the way." It was welcome news.

I quickly acted on the cop's advice, then I went back to where Rachel lay. She was still unconscious. I didn't dare move her any farther until the professionals arrived. I found her bathroom and grabbed a towel. Then I went back to her. I pressed the towel against the wound to help stop the bleeding. It didn't look as if she had lost much blood.

Presently I heard a siren, and the sound of brakes outside. A few seconds later, there was a loud knock on the door. I wondered why they didn't just come in, and then I remembered that I had locked all the entrances.

I quickly got up from the floor next to Rachel, unlocked the door, and realized it was Andrew Dark, the same helpful uniformed cop from before at the police station.

"She's right over here." I said as I realized that he had to see her. She was only a few feet from the door. "Is the ambulance on its way?" Before the other man could speak I heard another siren, and was suddenly relieved.

After administering first aid and gently placing the still unconscious woman on a stretcher, the attendants wheeled her out to the waiting ambulance. Soon the siren again pierced the air as the emergency vehicle quickly departed the scene.

Just then another cop appeared out of the nearby trees. In his hand was a cartridge shell. "He fired from right back there." He related. "He used a rifle. At such close range you were lucky you or the lady weren't killed".

After taking my statement the two cops left, leaving me to wonder what the hell was going on? I was getting tired of being threatened, and then shot at. Just what had I gotten myself into?

Chapter Nine

I decided it was time I got some answers from my employer. I wanted to stick around Richmond for a few days anyway, to see if Rachel would recover from her wound. She'd gotten a bad break when I knocked on her door.

I called the number Jeremy Taylor had given me. After a few rings, a woman answered.

"Hello?"

I was thrown off a little, hearing a female voice. "I was given this number to reach Jeremy Taylor. Is he there?"

The voice on the other end of the line was pleasant enough, "No. This is his secretary. May I take a message?"

"I really need to speak with Mr. Taylor. When will he be available?"

"If you are Mr. Dunn, I've been instructed to take all your information. You can be sure I will pass it on promptly."

"Okay," I said, and hoped my irritability didn't show up on the other end of the line. I told her what I had found out so far, and that I would be detained for a few days in Richmond before heading into Texas to pick up the trail of Phillip Atchison the third. She asked politely if it would be necessary for me to delay my search, and I said yes, but I would not bill them for the personal time. She seemed satisfied with my explanation. When I hung up I felt strangely relieved.

The Shenandoah General Hospital was across town from the hotel, so I drove the rental car. I was just in time for afternoon visiting hours. It seemed my luck was changing. I checked on Rachel's room at the information center in the lobby, then caught the elevator up to the third floor. When I passed the nurse's station there were three women in white there. I thought that might be a good sign; no emergencies.

The door to Rachel's room was open so I walked in. I was surprised to see her sitting up in bed reading a magazine.

"I thought this place was for sick people." I said, casually.

"You're still here. I thought you might have left town." She sounded excited and happy to see me. I wasn't used to that.

"I had to make sure you were all right. You didn't look too good the last time I saw you."

"Come sit on the bed next to me."

It was the best invitation I'd had in a long time, so I complied. Instinctively I took her right hand. The other arm was in a sling. She didn't pull away. I was feeling better, and I wasn't even sick. "What does the doctor say? Are you stuck in here for a while?"

"Well let's see," she looked thoughtful. "This is Saturday and the man in the white coat says I only have to stay another two days, so I should be out Monday."

"Your math is really good." I kidded. "Then what happens?"

Her eyes drifted to the open window, and she looked a little sad. "I'm not sure. I don't want to go back home with a psycho on the loose. So I-----"

I interrupted her. "I don't think you have to worry. I'm convinced the gunman was after me. I've been nosing around town asking a lot of questions. Maybe I struck a nerve with someone."

"That doesn't make sense to me." She said. "What could you possibly have found that would make a person want to kill you?"

"It's even less plausible that someone would want to harm you." I didn't say it but I was thinking that she was so pretty they'd want to kiss her to death, not shoot her. Instinctively I squeezed her hand.

Rachel noticed the pressure but she didn't react one way or the other. She said, "I haven't thanked you yet for saving my life. The policeman told me how you pulled me out of the line of fire."

I changed the subject. Surprisingly I was a little embarrassed. "So if you don't go back to your house, where will you stay?"

She gently pulled her right hand from mine. "I was thinking that I might ask my aunt in Muncie if I can move in with her for a while, just until I get into another place of my own. She's all alone since her husband didn't come back from the war. I wouldn't want to be there permanently though. I will need more room for when my son comes home."

"Wait a minute!" I was really thrown off guard. "You have a child?"

"Well he's not a child really. He's almost twenty."

I wanted to ask if she'd ever been married, but was afraid. It had to have happened about the time Phillip the third disappeared.

She anticipated what I was thinking. "Flip, that's what I called Phillip, is my son's father! So you see I'm not as pure as you might think."

"I like to think that I'm not judgmental. Besides, you were in love with the guy. You told me that."

"Yes I was. When he came to see me that last day, he was really upset, as you might imagine. I tried to comfort him, and things just escalated from there. He was crying the whole time. I'm not sorry it happened. He's been my only love, and I've got a great son that I'm proud of." As she was finishing, her eyes were glistening, and a tear made its way down her high-boned cheek. She wiped it away quickly.

I reached for her hand again, gently. "I'm not judging, Rachel. I hope I can find him for you. What is your son's name?"

"Thomas. Thomas Embree," she replied, with just a hint of pride in her voice. He's somewhere overseas, in the Army. I haven't heard from him in a while and with this Korean thing going on, I'm worried."

It seemed important somehow that I should comfort her. "If anything had happened to him, you would be notified. The military is very good about those things. It's natural for a mother to worry, but I'm sure he's okay."

Right then the nurse came in and sent me out of the room. Before leaving I assured Rachel that I would be back before she was released, but that I had some things to attend to first. Something she had said before just struck me, and I needed to check it out.

I drove to the police station, which was back toward the hotel. I wanted to see if Andrew Dark could straighten out a discrepancy in something I'd been told.

I was informed that he was there, but he was busy with someone else. I told the desk sergeant that I would wait. I found a seat near the front window, and spent the next few minutes looking out at the street, and the passersby. As it turned out I had a short wait.

When Dark emerged from a room near the front desk he saw me. He smiled and walked over to where I sat. "I was hoping I'd run into you. How's Miss Embree doing?"

"She's coming right along. She thinks she'll be released to go home on Monday." I didn't mention the fact that she didn't want to return to her house. "Any news on the shooter?"

"Nothing yet, except that the shell casing we found at the scene came from an Italian make rifle." He looked in my eyes to see if the news meant anything to me. It didn't, not then anyway.

"Actually I came to ask you two things. Are you any relation to Alvin Dark the Giants baseball player? I've heard he comes from down here somewhere."

"That's an easy one. No I'm not, but I wish I had his money." He replied. "What's your second question?"

Now the important one, the answer that made it worthwhile to wait for. I stood up in anticipation. "I'm confused. You said that the FBI report stated that four shots were fired from the recovered pistol. Right?"

"That's correct." He answered.

"But you also inferred that only two shots were fired in the bank. So what happened to the other two bullets?"

"I have no idea." He replied. "When the FBI took over the investigation, we went on to other cases. I never thought about that until you just brought it up."

I didn't want to tell him the story Rachel had told me about what really happened in the bank. I wanted to make sure she was in the clear, as far as aiding and abetting. I didn't think of it as my responsibility. I thanked him for his time and left.

My next stop would be the city library. That seemed to be about as good a place as any to locate the address of the two Lambrights. It would have to wait until the next day though. I was beat. The hotel bed sounded like the best move for me. Then I remembered that tomorrow was Sunday, and the library wouldn't be open. I would have to get there before it closed that day.

The librarian lady was very helpful, all smiling. She led me to the phone book section quietly, did a slight bow, and went back to her desk.

I was in my third town before I found what I was looking for. Interestingly enough it was in Muncie, the same place Rachel had mentioned that she might relocate to. It was listed under the name of Lambright, Rodney J. I was hoping there wasn't more than one of them. I jotted down the address on a piece of paper I had in my wallet, nodded my thanks to the helpful lady behind the desk, and walked back to my car. Then it hit me that I had no idea where Muncie was. Damn, I would have to see Rachel again.

Chapter Ten

She wasn't in her room when I entered. I worried that something might be wrong. Then the bathroom door opened and, amazingly, the room was transformed into a place of beauty. 'watch it fella' I said to myself, 'you'll turn into a damn poet.' She was obviously having an effect on me.

"Hello," she said, beaming. "What brings you back to my humble abode?"

"I was in the neighborhood, so I thought I'd drop by and bring you flowers. Uh, oh, I forgot the flowers." I said, I hoped cutely. If I was going to give her something, it wouldn't be a present that would die.

"Funny." She smiled, and it was almost a laugh. Then her face took on a serious look. "Has something happened?"

I looked in her eyes, taking it all in. God she was beautiful, and so helpless looking in her hospital gown. "No, I just wanted to see you." It was true. "And I need some directions. I have to go to Muncie, and I have no idea where it is." We both knew that I could have gotten a map.

She saw right through that one. "Once you get to Indiana, it's not hard to find."

"You're amusing too," I laughed. She wasn't hard to talk to. We made small talk for a while, and when I left I kissed her on the forehead. I didn't have to bend down, as tall as she was.

I got a good night's sleep and Sunday I found the road to Muncie easily enough, following Rachel's directions. It was a two-lane road that must have seen better days. Dodging potholes was not easy. After forty miles or so I could see the town ahead. Just then a sign on the right proclaimed the population, eleven hundred. It was a metropolis. I saw a gas station on the right, so I stopped and bought a map. The address that I had found in the phonebook was not too far away.

After a few minutes I approached a large brick house. There was no number on the mailbox, but it had to be the place I was looking for. The porch in front of the house that was set back from the road about sixty feet looked more like a deck. It was huge. There was a redwood railing that separated it from the green grass lawn that, I supposed, would take a power mower to keep up with. Off to the left of the house was a three-car garage. Everything I saw seemed overly extravagant. The bell beside the mahogany door was different. It was in the form of a large fist, made of bronze. As I pushed it I could hear music inside the house. "For Christ's sake," I said to no one in particular because it seemed so ridiculous at the time. "Maybe they will put a man on the moon." As I waited I stepped back and moved so as to view the yard.

As the door opened I turned around, and was surprised to see the little bald guy, minus the gun. A shocked look appeared on his face as he recognized me. I took two quick steps toward him and grabbed his starched white shirt with both hands just below the collar. I shoved him against the door jamb hard. He grunted and tried to pull away, but I was too strong for him. I pulled him away from the door and slammed his body into an adjacent wall. He was still trying to break my grip when I heard a woman's voice from inside the house.

"Is this a private dance, or can anyone join?"

She was standing at the foot of a large staircase that circled up to what I presumed to be the bedroom floor. I relaxed my grip on the little runt, and said. "There's a reason for this. He threatened me with a gun. I'm just settling the score."

As the man backed away from me, I let him go, but watched him carefully. "Who are you people?"

"I thought you knew, since you broke into our home," the woman of the house said.

"I came to see Rodney Lambright. Is that him?" I asked pointing toward the man, who had sat down in a large chair across the expansive room.

"Call the cops, Louise. We don't have to put up with this!" It was the first thing the guy had said.

Now I was surprised. "Are you Louise Ormsby?" I questioned, turning my full attention to the woman on the stairs. She didn't look anything like Rachel had described her. Of course that had been the teen-age version. This was a full-blown woman. She had a couple of streaks of gray in her long dark brown hair. It was rather becoming. She didn't look as short as I had pictured, but then she was standing on the bottom step of her stairs. She wore a light green dress that was form-fitting and very flattering, showing off her considerable bosom and slim waist. She was wearing nylons and high-heeled shoes that matched her dress. Her face showed signs of wear, but even with her character-line wrinkles, or cat paws, around her eyes, she was very attractive, with full red lips, and a slightly turned-up nose.

She interrupted my surveillance, "correction. The name is Lambright. I'm married to your dance partner. I haven't been an Ormsby for almost twenty years."

"Actually I wanted to talk to you both, and maybe we can clear up any misunderstanding about why I'm here."

"That would be nice." She answered. "I don't really want to call the police, but I don't want my husband to have a heart attack either"

By the tone of her voice when she said husband, like it would choke her, I gathered they weren't very close. "I've been hired to find Phillip Atchison the third."

"Who hired you?" She asked. Rodney, if that's who he was, sat up in his chair, suddenly interested.

"I'm not sure." She was at least cordial, so I didn't mind answering her. "The man who paid me was named Jeremy Taylor, but I think he was just a go-between."

"That was over twenty years ago. Why would someone be interested now, after all that time?" Rodney had finally weighed into our conversation. Now we were getting somewhere.

"I have no idea, but they gave me a list of people who might be able to help. Both your names were on it." I waited for a reaction. Reading their body language would have been easier if they were standing together, but instead Louise stayed by the stairs, while Rodney was seated far across the room. I concentrated on the little man. He gave no hint of what he might be thinking.

When he spoke he seemed more under control. "I don't know how we could help. The last time we saw Phillip was at school the day my father was killed."

"How about you Louise? You can speak for yourself I presume." I said as I turned in her direction.

"No. That's right. I was in his class, and I wanted to talk to him, but he hurried out so fast that I didn't get a chance. I thought we had a date to go to the movies that night, but he didn't even bother to leave me a note. He just never showed up." As she spoke she walked to a position near me. "Do you have any leads?"

I didn't want to bring Rachel into our conversation, so I said "No. Nothing more than the newspaper articles about that day."

Rodney seemed to flinch, and his gaze wandered to a nearby wall where a large cabinet stood. Behind its glass front were several rifles and handguns. I couldn't help but notice that one of the rifles was missing. "What's with all the guns?" I just flat-out asked. Nothing like being direct.

"They were my father's. I was awarded them in his will." Now he seemed nervous again.

"Did the gun you threatened me with come from those?" I pointed to the cabinet.

"Yes, but it wasn't loaded." Rodney answered.

"But I didn't know that. Where's the rifle that's missing."

He hesitated before speaking, "We had a break-in and it was stolen."

"Oh, that was convenient. When did that happen?" I said, thinking of the woman with a hole in her shoulder.

Rodney looked at his wife. She waved her arm as if to signal that it was his story, and he would have to answer.

"Never mind. It will be easy to check the police report." I wanted to see him squirm. I was sure he'd never reported it, if there even was a robbery.

He confirmed my suspicions. "It was the only thing taken, so we didn't want to be drawn into a police investigation. We didn't report it."

"Okay. I have one more question before I leave. Why did you come to my room asking questions?" I looked directly at Rodney Lambright.

He didn't answer right away, and Louise walked toward the door saying, "I think that's enough answers for one day, Mr. Dunn is it? You should leave now."

So I left, not much smarter than when I got there, except for now I knew where the rifle came from, and probably the German Luger used in the bank killings.

Chapter Eleven

It was dark when Phillip left Rachel. It was a night with no moon, or it was obscured by clouds. He couldn't tell which. He didn't want to leave, but he felt he had no choice. He left her laying on the bed that had held the consummation of their love for one another. Rachel's father was due home any minute, so there was an urgency to his departure.

She'd been so beautiful, with the sheet pulled up to her chin. It was a bittersweet ending to the worst day of his life. He wondered what she thought of him. He couldn't stop crying, whimpering actually. He tried to be a man but he couldn't pull it off.

His father was dead! He was a fugitive, who most likely would be charged with the killing. Another man had lost his life at Phillip's own hand.

Rachel had tried to comfort him, and it got out of hand. He was clumsy and inexperienced. It was his first time. She helped as best she could, but it hurt her when he tried entering her. He could feel blood on his leg. Then as they kissed, there was a tenderness between them as they both realized that they had moved past puppy love.

Now as he stealthily made his way down the dark street he was glad he was alone. There was no place for Rachel in what he had to do. Later, when the furor had died down, perhaps he could return and things would be as they had always been. But that was crazy. Would his father spring back to life? Would the other man, whoever he was, be alive and forgive him? No. He would never go to college, never be a writer.

He broke into a trot. It was only a few blocks to the railroad tracks. He had seen freight cars parked along the side-rails when he had come to visit Rachel. He would hide in one of them until he could find one heading out of town.

He was in luck. There was a freight car far enough away from the station that he might not be detected. Suddenly he was very tired. The events of the day were piling up on him, and the weariness weakened his legs. He just needed to get off his feet.

The door to the boxcar was open wide. He pulled himself up onto the car's platform, scraping his right knee as he did so. It was extremely dark inside the big car. He felt along the metal side until he found a corner, and collapsed, exhausted.

He was awakened by a clanging sound. He realized quickly that it was the huge metal door of the boxcar slamming shut. He drifted quickly back to sleep.

The next time he awoke it was to the sound of someone whispering. He thought he was dreaming. It took a minute for him to realize that the sound of voices was coming from inside the boxcar, and he was indeed awake. Then he noticed something else; the train was moving.

A gravelly, deep voice that seemed very near boomed out of the darkness that surrounded Phillip. "Well. Look what we got here; a baby boy."

His eyes were slowly becoming accustomed to the dark, and he could see what appeared to be a large shadow standing in front of him.

The voice spoke again. "You got any money boy?"

"No." Phillip answered. He was becoming afraid. He might not have been so worried, had he remembered the gun tucked into his waistband just above the crack of his buttocks.

"Let's search him." It was a new voice from across the car. This one sounded high pitched and younger.

Someone grabbed him by the arm. He tried to pull away, but his assailant was too strong.

He heard rustling as the other voice came closer. "You got him?"

"Let the kid alone!" It was a third voice, A very strong, loud one.

"You stay out of this, Redbird. It ain't none of your business," gravelly voice said.

"Well, I'm making it my business. You're scaring the boy. He's not bothering you."

"I said butt out. He's in our car and he's got to pay his share." The first assailant said, belligerently.

"Yeah," the weaker voice chimed in.

Phillip could see all of them now, but only as silhouettes. The one called Redbird had gotten up, and grabbed the arm of the smaller of the two men. He yanked him away so hard that he fell onto the bed of the car, making a clanging noise as he did so. He made no attempt to get up.

"I said stop!" he commanded, louder now. Suddenly the bigger man let go of Phillip, who fell back onto the seat of his pants. He too stayed put.

"I'll remember this, Redbird," he muttered, walking back to the other side of the car.

"Are you okay kid?" Phillip's benefactor asked, as he leaned over him.

"Yes, thank you, but my arm hurts a little." Thank you seemed a little weak to the boy though, because he might have been killed, had not the man called Redbird intervened.

The man, who appeared in the shadows to be an Indian said nothing. He moved to the metal door of the car, and grabbing the handle with both hands, he opened it wide. Sunlight streamed into the bed of their space, revealing them all.

Redbird wore no hat and had black hair pulled back and tied with something that looked like string. He had bushy eyebrows and a darkly tanned face. He was obviously an Indian, a tall, muscular one. He wore a collarless brown shirt open to reveal a chest with no hair.

Phillip let his gaze wander to the other two men, who were seated by the far wall of the train car. The first thing he noticed was their clothes, which were tattered and dingy. One man was fat and tall, while the other was just the opposite; short and skinny. They both wore hats, and were obviously white, in contrast with the Indian. They were pale and sickly looking.

The landscape outside was sliding by rapidly as the train must have reached full speed. Their car was shaking and bouncing, almost in tune with the clicking sound of the rails.

Redbird moved to the wall opposite the door, lied down on the rust-laden floor, and closed his eyes. Phillip didn't dare try to sleep, still fearing the other two passengers. He continued watching the scenery outside the open door. Soon the Indian began to snore softly, obviously asleep.

The boy could hear whispering between the two men across the car, but he couldn't tell what they were saying to one another. They both rose quietly and approached the sleeping man. The big one had something in his hand. It appeared to be a club, or a piece of metal. It was only about a foot long. Whatever it was, he swung it over his head and hit his adversary right in the midsection. Before the Indian could react he was hit on the side of his head, right above the ear. Falling back flat onto the floor, he lost consciousness.

Up to this point Phillip had done nothing, but he knew it would be just a matter of time before the two thugs attacked him. But what could he do? Suddenly he remembered the gun in his waistband. He reached behind him, and tugged the Luger free. He stood up, pointing it in the direction of the attackers. The light streaming in from the door of the big boxcar illuminated the weapon in his hand.

"Leave him alone!" Phillip screamed.

The big man turned toward the boy with the gun, and took a step toward him saying, "What are you going to do with that water pistol boy?"

"Just let us be!" Phillip's gun hand was shaking.

It was the big man again, "You're not going to take this dumb redskin's side against us are you?"

Before Phillip could answer, the smaller man yelled "Get him!"

Just then the train lurched around a curve in the tracks, and the big man rushed Phillip. The last thing he heard was the sound of the explosion, as the bullet tore through his chest, and out his back. He fell to the dusty, rust-covered bed of the car, twitching at first, and then still, his eyes open but unseeing.

The boy turned toward the only assailant left. He waved his gun hand toward the open door. "Jump." He said, calmer now.

"You're crazy. I ain't going to jump. The train's going way too fast."

Phillip's answer was, "One way or another you're getting off this train right here, right now." He pointed the gun in the little man's direction again. In his waning innocence he hadn't bothered to check to see how many bullets were left in the unfamiliar gun.

"Okay, I'll go," the man said, as he moved toward the open door. Then he turned, and rushed Phillip. Again the gun exploded in the boy's hand, and his assailant fell at his feet. Phillip grabbed the wounded man's arm and, pulling him toward the opening, he shoved him out onto the ground, which had to be rushing by at fifty miles an hour. He didn't bother looking to see where he had shot the man. The fall would surely kill him.

Phillip glanced at the Indian. The injured man had not awakened. Next he went to the big man he had shot who lay motionless on the floor. After placing the handgun back into his waistband, he rolled the body toward the freight-car's door. With one more shove the man fell onto the rocks beside the tracks.

It occurred to Phillip that the Indian didn't see what had happened after he was knocked unconscious. All he had to do was get rid of the gun, which he did by placing it in a dark corner away from Redbird. He doubted that it would be seen there. He took care to wipe the gun clean beforehand.

Funny, he thought, how one's life can change in just a few hours. Less than two days ago he was an innocent schoolboy, happy with his life. Since then he'd had his first encounter with sex, and now he was a cold-blooded killer running from the law. It was then that he realized he would never see Rachel again, and the boy in him began to sob.

Chapter Twelve

"What happened?" The Indian was awake now.

"You got hit over the head. You've been out for over an hour." Phillip knew what was coming next.

"Where are the other two?" Redbird glanced around,

"They jumped off when the train slowed a ways back." He had worked that out in his mind.

"Good riddance. Was it the big guy who hit me?" Phillip nodded in the affirmative. "I thought so. The other one was a coward." Redbird answered.

"I thought they were your friends." Phillip said.

Redbird looked at him quizzically, and then answered, "Naw. I met them in a camp back by where we picked up the train. We were just going the same way."

That made Phillip feel a little better. He liked this big stranger somehow, and didn't want to think he was cut from the same cloth as the other two.

"How come you're okay?"

Phillip thought quickly, "I think they were worried that you might come to."

The Indian walked over to something that was lying on the floor, and picking it up said, "One of them even left his hat. I must be scarier than I thought." He laughed, and then tossed it out the open door.

He held out his hand to Phillip, saying, "My name is Charlie Redbird, who are you?"

The boy hesitated just slightly. "I'm Jeb Lee," He said, taking the big fellow' s huge paw. He had combined the names of two of the south's greatest heroes; Jeb Stuart, and Robert E. Lee. This then would be a new start- a new life. He could only hope that it would be better than the one he had just left behind.

Charlie had the feeling that Jeb had saved him from at least a severe beating, and possibly much worse, but he didn't question him further. The boy obviously didn't want to talk about it. The Indian had learned long ago to just take things as they come, that they were fated to turn out the way they did.

"Where are you headed Charlie?" Jeb said.

"A place you've probably never heard of, Nacogdoches, Texas."

He was right. "Where in blazes is that?" Jeb was interested.

It's a little town in the northeast part of the state. I was offered a job there in the oil fields. I'm going to see if the offer still stands. How about you?"

Jeb hadn't given his destination any thought up until then. He just needed to get away. 'I'm not sure. I know I'll need to get a job right away. I'm pretty hungry."

Charlie reached into a bag over where he had been laying. "I can help with that part, at least for now, I brought along a couple of sandwiches." He handed one to Jeb.

This was how it was to be. It seemed they were always hungry or thirsty as they made their way by train and car and foot westward through the southern states into the Lone Star State. They did odd jobs along the way. They found streams to quench their thirst. There were helpful people on their journey who gave them rides, mostly short ones. And all the time they stayed together, this unlikely pair, who had shown their true colors to the other by lending a helping hand when it seemed most needed.

When they finally arrived in Nacogdoches, they were surprised by all the activity. Word of the stock market crash and subsequent depression had reached them on the road, so they didn't expect to find a boom town, but that's what it was. The discovery of oil had transformed the tiny cow town into a bustling community.

Charlie headed for the oil fields while Jeb, having decided to try his hand at being a cowboy, went looking for a ranch to see about a job. They figured on meeting back up again in town a few days later, hopefully both with good news.

It turned out the nearest ranch was five miles out of town, and Jeb walked the whole way, not having benefit of any other form of transportation. His shoes had more than one hole in them, so his socks became torn too. He was still wearing the clothes Rachel had provided from her father's closet. That seemed so long ago, but it had only been three weeks. The cool November air chilled him as he walked, giving him shivers.

After nearly three miles he was heartened by the sight of fences. Surely it wouldn't be long before a ranch house would appear on the horizon. He was right. A large barn-red structure sat on the right side of a smaller road that angled off about a half-mile farther down. He noticed a fenced corral next to the house, set back from the entrance road.

A man riding a horse approached from behind the corral. "Whoa boy," he said in a talkative tone, to his ride. "Are you a tenderfoot?" He asked, looking at Jeb.

Jeb didn't know what the cowboy was talking about, and answered, "A what?"

"You must be, if you don't even know what it is. You'll find the foreman behind the main house, in a shed. You picked a good time to show up." The cowboy, who didn't look much older than Jeb, turned his horse away, and spurred him slightly. The brown horse responded in a slow gait toward the road.

The cowboy had been right. It was a good time to ask for work. The oil boom had created hundreds of jobs, both in the fields, and at the ranches to replace the hands who had left for better money. Jeb got an advance on his pay to bankroll a cowhand's wardrobe, and even though he had no experience, he was treated very well, considering his age.

It wasn't long before the young cowboy became an old hand. There were many hired after him, and some had the same lack of experience.

On a rare day off, he finally ventured into town, hoping to find Charlie and share stories. They had decided before they split up to meet at the only café in town at noon on Saturdays. If the other didn't show up, they would leave a message about when their next day off would be. Hopefully, that way they would sooner or later be able to hook up.

It turned out that Charlie had been there the week before, and wouldn't be able to return for a couple of weeks. Jeb was disappointed. He really wanted to go to the only speakeasy in the area, but didn't want to go alone. He had aged a lot since his confrontations on the train. His skin was more leathery–looking from the intense sun of Texas, and he had a few wrinkles around his eyes. His body was becoming hardened by the heavy work load of his job. His western garb allowed him to blend in. He hadn't made any friends at the ranch yet, mostly because he was working his tail off, trying to learn how to be a cowboy, and keep up with the older ranch hands. It was a lonely existence, and he thought of Rachel often. At one of those times he wrote her a letter.

Chapter Thirteen

I decided it was time to share what I had learned at the Lambright's with Andrew Dark. I stopped by the police station on my way to my hotel room. Dark wasn't there at the time, but he was expected back soon. I didn't wait. My information would keep. It had been stored away for some twenty-odd years, so another day wouldn't matter. But the idea of the impact on Rodney Lambright and his wife was intriguing. At the very least, the fact that they hadn't reported the rifle stolen could come back to haunt them, especially if, as I suspected, it turned out to be the attempted murder weapon.

At the hotel desk I was informed that a Miss Rachel Embree had called, and would I please come to the hospital as soon as it was convenient.

It was the best offer I had had all day. I could sleep anytime. So I passed up on my soft bed and headed back out to see the beautiful dark haired one.

She was sitting up in the hospital bed when I came through her door. Her smile warmed me immediately. "It took you long enough. I left the message for you at least twenty minutes ago."

She was playing with me. That was a good sign. "Well, aren't you perky today?"

"I have some good news. I heard from Thomas. He's on his way home. Isn't that wonderful?" She was beaming.

"That is great news. Now you won't have to be alone. How soon will he be here?"

"He's in Tokyo right now waiting for a military flight out. I think they call it MATS. It should only be a few days. The people I talked to told me he might even be able to get a hardship discharge, because of my circumstances, the attempt on my life."

"Do you think that's what he wants?" I asked, remembering the camaraderie I felt in the service during World War two. It might be the same during the Korean thing.

She looked thoughtful, "I'll certainly ask him. I don't want to be the cause of anything that would affect his life in a negative way. It would be nice if he was home for more than a few days. I know that's just a mother talking though."

I was impressed with her selflessness. "I'm sure it will all work out," I said agreeably. "Now maybe you won't have to move to that other town, and you can go back to your own place."

"Well I certainly will at first." Then she added, "But I may be released tomorrow, and Thomas surely won't be back by then. Do you think that maybe you could stay at the house until he returns?" There was a plaintive look on her face.

I was flattered. It was what I was hoping for. "Only if I can sleep on your couch." It was the gentlemanly statement to make, even though I knew that's what she meant.

She looked flustered. "I would like that."

"Look Rachel, there's a lot going on right now, and I want to do anything I can to help. I've already called the people who hired me to clear my schedule for a few days. I don't see what difference a little more time can make." And I added, "Besides, you're nice to look at, and I don't want it to end." I was afraid I had overstepped propriety, but she put me at ease by laughing.

"That's what I need on my couch, a Casanova."

Now I was the one who was embarrassed. "Sorry, sometimes I say what I'm thinking. It gets me in trouble."

With perfect timing the nurse entered. "I'm sorry young man. You'll have to leave so we can do our work."

I didn't want to go, but I said, "I need to follow up on a few things anyway," and I reached over, took Rachel's hand and gently kissed her on the forehead. "Get some sleep. I'll be back tomorrow."

Rachel nodded agreeably, and yawned as if on cue. Even then she was pretty, but I didn't tell her. I walked out, looking forward to Monday for the first time in a long while.

It was getting late, but since I knew that my helpful police friend was working on Sunday and I was out and about anyway, I decided to check back in at the police station. This time I got lucky and Andrew Dark was there. I asked him if he had time for a cup of coffee, and he answered in the affirmative. We went down the street to the café I had been to before. Once we were seated I told him what I had seen at the Lambrights.

"I'll definitely have to follow up on that. You say they didn't report a break in?" Dark questioned.

"That's what Rodney Lambright told me, after I brought it up. I think he knows that the missing rifle was the weapon used in the attempt on my or Rachel Embree's life."

When the waitress came, I just ordered coffee, while Dark spent two minutes picking out a whole meal from the huge menu. "I need a big meal. I've had a long day." He said in answer to the surprised look on my face. He was a slim guy, maybe one-forty packed on his less than six foot frame. I wondered where he put it all.

"Well that will do it. I hope there's enough food left in the kitchen for Monday." I smiled.

"Back to the business at hand," he began. What do you think of the Lambrights?"

"I think they're a strange couple. I wonder how they got together?" Strange was a mild word. They were weird.

The cop looked thoughtful and then spoke, as if measuring his words carefully. "Of course they were in high school together. She left town for a while after graduation, and when she came back she had a baby and a marriage certificate." He looked in my eyes to see my reaction.

I was shocked. Not because of the baby, or the obvious circumstances, but because no one had mentioned a child up until then. "A baby? What happened to it?" It is what I use to describe a child when I don't know the gender.

"It was a boy. They named him Harold. He's still around. He works at the local newspaper." Dark answered.

I thought about the smart-mouthed kid who had greeted me the day I came to town. "He can't be more than nineteen or twenty. How could he make reporter so young?"

"He's not really a reporter, just a gopher. He'd like everyone to think he's important though."

There was something nagging at me, but I couldn't bring it out into the daylight. It seemed important somehow. Oh well, maybe it will come to me, I thought.

I didn't wait around for my officer friend to eat his humongous meal. I was getting weary. My hotel bed seemed like a good destination to finish out the day.

Chapter Fourteen

Monday was destined to become my favorite day. I could feel it. I awoke early, about five A.M, and I had a smile on my face. You have to understand that I don't smile much. By the time I showered and dressed it was six. I walked over to the café where I had met Andrew Dark the night before. I probably wouldn't be able to get in to see Rachel until nine, so when the waitress came I ordered a full breakfast, with juice, bacon and eggs, scrambled so I could put hot sauce on them. Pepper just didn't do it for me. I needed most of my food to be spicy and hot. I wondered often if I had a little Mexican or Spanish blood in me. I didn't like Greek food. It was too bland.

After breakfast I ordered a refill on my twenty-five cent coffee, found a newspaper, and casually glanced through it, watching the big clock on the wall every minute or so.

At ten to nine I drove to the hospital. I didn't want to waste a minute that I could be spending with Rachel. I guess you could say that I was smitten. I had no idea how she felt about me. I know she thought I had saved her life. But I was sure the gunman had wanted to kill me, because I might be getting too close to finding out something I wasn't supposed to, something that could put the attempted killer in jeopardy. It was a bold move, so whatever secret he or she wanted to keep hidden must have been a whopper.

When I arrived at Rachel's room she was still in bed, sitting up, and staring out the window. She turned toward me as I entered, and her welcoming smile lit up the room. At least it did for me.

"Good morning, my protector." It was an obvious reference to the other day when we were in danger.

"Hi." I answered back, eloquently. "How's the invalid feeling today?"

"Let me put it this way. The sky is more blue out my window. The birds in the courtyard are singing my song. And even the hospital food tastes good."

"I didn't know you were a poet. That's just one more interesting facet of your personality." I answered.

"So what's going on in the real world this glorious morning?" She questioned, the smile still frozen on her face.

"I came to help you get out of this place. Is it still today?" I said hopefully.

96

She swung her trim legs to the side of the bed toward the window, away from me. I caught a glimpse of her tanned back under her hospital gown, which was parted slightly.

Rachel was oblivious to the show she was putting on for me. "The doctor is supposed to be here around ten to release me. I'll have to wear this sling for a few more days, but it's not too inconvenient." Suddenly she became aware that her gown was open in the back, and she turned back, pulling the covers over her legs. She blushed, looking at me.

I answered her obvious question, "I'm not complaining that you turned away from me. I kind of enjoyed it."

"You are a scoundrel aren't you?" She said playfully, no longer embarrassed.

It was more like eleven when the doctor finally showed up. He told Rachel that everything looked good, after examining her shoulder, and told her to go ahead and get dressed while he informed the nurse's station, and signed the necessary release papers. I was asked courteously to leave the room.

After what seemed like a half-hour a fully dressed Rachel emerged and asked me to retrieve her overnight bag, which was still in the closet of her room. We took the elevator to the first floor, where she left her wheelchair, and we walked together out into the sunlight.

She waited in front of the hospital entrance while I went to the parking garage for my rental car.

When we arrived at her house I helped her out of the car, taking care not to hit her arm on anything. Once inside she placed herself on her couch, heaving a sigh of relief. "It's so good to finally be home." She said, a little breathlessly.

"I don't think anyone will bother you while I'm here." I wanted to reassure her. I didn't think about the fact that I was with Rachel when the first attempt happened.

"I do feel better with you here." She answered, and then said thoughtfully, "It's funny. I've only known you for a few days, but I'm perfectly comfortable being with you. You weren't a priest in some other life, were you?"

I laughed, "More like the opposite, I'd say."

We made small talk, as friends do, for the rest of the day. I made lunch for her with what I could find in her pantry and refrigerator. I thought she might need help feeding herself, but she did very well. When it came time for dinner I was prepared to do it again, but she suggested we go out to eat-her treat. I didn't let her pay, but we did go to a nice restaurant not too far away. We had a candle-lit booth, and the food was good. It seemed as if we were on a date, and we even became a little self-conscious with each other, like two people who were trying to impress the other with their restraint, and good manners. When I brought her home, it was all I could do not to kiss her on her lips when we reached her doorstep. As I opened Rachel's door I had that strange feeling you sometimes get when you are being watched. I turned around, but saw nothing.

Chapter Fifteen

After leaving Jeb Lee to find his way to a nearby ranch, Charlie Redbird hitched a ride to the oilfields. He found the foreman at one of the dozen or so rigs within sight. The man hired the big Indian on the spot. He was given an advance on his salary to buy clothes, and was on the job the next day. There were a few other laborers of Indian heritage at the fields, most of them Cherokees like him. The work was hard and long. Most nights he fell into his bed in the company bunkhouse and was asleep in minutes. He planned to get back into town and share stories with his newfound friend Jeb as soon as possible, but it would at least have to be after payday.

Charlie knew that his family came from Oklahoma. Before his father was killed the older man shared the story of how he had met the boy's mother, and the tragedy that ensued.

It was eighteen ninety-nine, and there was great anticipation at the dawn of the new century. Charlotte Amundsen, a Norwegian immigrant had arrived in the town of Shawnee, Oklahoma with her intended James

Hardy, a hot-headed Irishman. Hardy was a small man, not much taller than Charlotte. He had a reputation in Minnesota for starting fights for little reason. He was a fierce combatant, and though he often ended up bruised, he stayed alive. Luckily none of his adversaries wore guns. The one person Hardy was civil with was Charlotte, whom he had met through an acquaintance that he worked with at a local tannery. The young twenty year old girl was attracted to the small, but muscular gentleman. She had no idea of his temper.

Charlotte was not a really pretty girl. She wore her hair Scandinavian style, tight to her head and in braids. She was about five feet tall, with full breasts, and a slightly thick waist. Her teeth were uneven from neglect. She did have wide eyes with eyebrows that were not bushy at all. She had come from a lower class family that had come to America in steerage. They were domestics who were allowed to live in the mansion of their employ, and paid a small stipend.

So it wasn't hard for the young Norwegian, who had been born in the States, and spoke good English, to fall for Hardy who she perceived to be a desirable mate.

Hardy inherited a considerable sum from his parents who caught typhoid and died within days of each other. It was then that he decided to move south. Charlotte agreed to go with him, assuming that they would soon be married.

The young couple moved from town to town for a while. James was looking for a business to provide them with a good living, before his inheritance ran out. They finally settled in Shawnee, Oklahoma, a reasonably small town near the Missouri border. A trading post there was for sale. It seemed like the perfect opportunity. They would both work there, and save the expense of hiring someone else.

Things went well at first. They both worked hard, and were fairly successful. They pooled their earnings and lived like man and wife in a small cabin next to the business. Charlotte was not unhappy. She waited for her man to talk of marriage, but the subject did not come up. Nor did a discussion about children.

One evening Charlotte decided to bring up the subject. She wanted a child, and since the store was doing well, she was becoming impatient. When Hardy made a will with her as beneficiary, she was sure he wanted the same thing; marriage and a child as soon as possible. He put her off saying it just wasn't the right time. She protested, and he stormed out without another word.

Late that night there was a persistent knock on the cabin door that woke her from a fitful sleep. She wondered why her man didn't just use his key. She grabbed her robe from a hook on the wall near her bed, and walking to the door and tying the belt around her waist at the same time she said, "Just a minute darling." She fumbled with the lock in the dark, and then opening the door she was surprised to see the town sheriff standing there.

"I have bad news Miss Charlotte. James was killed tonight!"

Charlotte's knees buckled and she almost collapsed. The sheriff reached out to steady her saying, "I'm sorry. Is there anything I can do? Do you want my wife to come stay with you?"

Holding back the tears, she replied, "No. I'll be all right. Thank you for the offer."

"We'll make all the arrangements, and my wife will be over to see how you're doing in a few days," the sheriff said considerately.

Almost immediately after the sheriff walked away and she closed the door, Charlotte realized that she hadn't asked for any particulars of her lover's demise. She thought about calling after the man, but then decided against it. She would find out tomorrow. She collapsed back on the bed, and then the tears came. She cried not so much for James, but for her predicament. What was she to do? At first she forgot that Hardy had executed a will in her favor, and she thought that she would lose her means of support. The realization that the trading post would be hers brought some relief, but only for a moment. She couldn't handle such an endeavor by herself, could she? Maybe by cutting back on store hours she would be able to manage it. She could learn the bookwork and ordering of supplies. It was nearly four in the morning when she finally fell asleep.

The next day, as luck would have it, it rained so hard that the dirt road in front of the store became a sea of mud. Charlotte donned her boots and made the trading post ready for business anyway. There was no time to mourn. People came by from time to time with condolence, and she was able to piece together what had happened to James Hardy the night before.

It seems he had gone into a local saloon, of which there were many, with a sour attitude. It didn't take long for him to antagonize one of the bar's customers. A fistfight started and soon escalated into something else. Someone pulled a gun. Only one shot was fired, but that bullet found the heart of James Hardy. Even as he fell mortally wounded, everyone ran for the door. No one could recall who fired the fatal shot.

For a while after the funeral the trading post did a brisk business. Charlotte dared to dream that things would be all right. It wasn't until that winter of the first year of the new century that sales took a downturn and Charlotte worried anew that she might have to sell the business.

It was then that a tall Indian came to the post looking for supplies. In those days many retailers would not do business with natives. Resentments still ran deep on both sides. Charlotte harbored none of the prejudices of the other whites and gladly filled the man's order. Because he was an oddity in town, she sized him up while retrieving the items on his list. In addition to being nearly six feet in height, he was a big man, but with a narrow waist. His shoulders were broad, his chest bulging more than his stomach. He had obvious native features, from his dark black shiny hair, which he wore in a traditional pony tail, to his bushy eyebrows which were also very dark. The only odd thing about the picture he presented was his clothes. They were more like everyone else in town. He wore tight-fitting dungarees and a plaid shirt open at the collar to reveal a hairless upper torso. He did wear more traditional moccasins. He appeared to be about thirty years of age.

Charlotte saw the big Indian again, but the circumstances were quite different. It was a very slow day at the trading post and she used the time to restock her shelves. She was in the back room when a sound out front alerted her to the possibility of a customer. As she emerged from the storage room someone grabbed her.

She couldn't move. Her assailant had encircled her arms. He was very strong. "I'll show you, you bitch, what happens to people who do business with savages," he grunted, dragging her into the back. The man shoved Charlotte to the floor and fell on top of her, trying to force her legs apart and pulling on her blouse at the same time.

The front door opened again. Charlotte heard it but had no way of knowing who had entered. She was losing the battle on the sawdust floor, trying to reach the assailant's eyes with one hand she had freed, but unsuccessful until then.

Suddenly the weight pressing her body to the floor lightened and then was gone, as her assailant was pulled forcibly from her. She raised herself on her elbows to see the Indian from before throwing the attacker against shelving on the wall. Pots and pans fell off the shelves as the two men struggled, Her assailant was trying to reach his holstered gun.

but by leaving his face open, the Indian was able to hit him with a roundhouse right fist that knocked the smaller man to the floor. He was about to jump him when a shot rang out.

They all looked toward the door to see the sheriff standing there with a smoking six-shooter, but none of them were hit.

"Do I have your attention?" The man with the badge shouted. No one answered, but they all were staring at him. Charlotte rose from the ground, unsteadily. The attacker stayed put at the feet of the big Indian. "I'll take your silence as a yes," the sheriff said.

"I want the two of you," he announced, looking at the two men, "to head on out to the jail. We'll let the judge sort this out when he gets here next month."

Charlotte spoke for the first time. "You can't do that Sheriff, the Indian was just protecting me. That thug on the floor attacked me!"

"His name is Andy, and I've had trouble with him before, so I'm inclined to believe you." The sheriff said looking at Charlotte. "But I don't know this big buck, so why should I believe that he's innocent?"

"I hope you'll take my word for it Sheriff. Why would I lie?" She answered, as she began dusting herself off.

"Well all right missus, but if any more trouble is caused by this Indian fella, I'll hold you responsible."

"Fair enough," she said.

And that's how it began. After the two men left the store, Charlotte thanked her savior. She found out his name was Henry Starr, and he was camped alone not far from town. He had a little money earned from odd jobs nearby.

She made coffee as they talked. Henry's English was good enough to be understood, but he only spoke in answer to her questions. She detected a wariness on his part to say too much. It was probably because he didn't trust her, she being white and all.

The blond woman, who was now all alone, made a quick decision. She needed help in the store, and he could use a little extra money. She was a little surprised when he agreed to come and work for her.

Chapter Sixteen

In the months that followed Charlotte and Henry grew close. When that fact became apparent to the good townsfolk of Shawnee the trading post business fell off drastically. It got to the point where they couldn't even earn enough to buy more supplies. They made a valiant effort, working longer hours, and selling some items at cost, but nothing worked. The clientele was so limited because of the prejudices that were produced by the protracted Indian wars.

When Charlotte realized that she was pregnant, they had no choice but to sell the store to the first bidder. She had received word from her older brother in Virginia that they could come live with he and his family until the baby was born.

Ludwig Amundsen missed his sister. He had been born in the old country, and had no preconceived ideas about the Indians who roamed the plains. He was willing to give anyone a chance. It would be good to have a little one in the house again. All of his children were in their teens, nearly ready to venture into the world alone.

Charlotte was beginning to show signs that she was with child when she and Henry Starr boarded the train for Richmond. They were sad that they had lost their business, but excited to begin a new life in the east.

Although they didn't marry, Henry doted on his pregnant lady. Ludwig had given the strong Indian a job in his lumber yard, and that allowed Charlotte to remain at home taking care of herself and helping to oversee the Amundsen children with Ludwig's wife Ariel.

On a mild day in June 1904, with the help of a midwife, a baby boy was born to Charlotte and Henry. She had gained nearly forty pounds throughout her pregnancy. It was too much. Though the child was saved, the mother did not survive. She just drifted away from the loss of blood.

Henry was devastated. His last rational act was to name his son Charles, after his wife. He gave the boy the last name of Redbird. It had been Charlotte's wish. She had loved watching birds outside her window. The distraught father began drinking heavily. Ludwig and his wife took over care of the child, as Henry was seldom home. He stopped showing up for work. He could not bring himself to look at

Charles, somehow blaming the child for Charlotte's death.

The Amundsen's received word that Henry had been killed on Charles second birthday. There'd been a fight in a saloon, and the big Indian's skull had been fractured. He died hours later in a hospital, having never regained conciousness.

Although the Norwegian couple petitioned the court for custody of Charles, it was decided that, because he was an Indian, the State should take over his care. So it was that he was sent to live in an institution much like a reform school. He was barely three years old.

By the time Charles was six he was so malnourished that he almost died. The sadistic headmaster at the school was skimming food money that the state provided, spending it on his own lavish whims. When the boy was finally transferred to the infirmary, a sympathetic nurse realized what was happening, and alerted State officials to what was going on. They promptly replaced the head man. Things improved immediately. For a while it became almost tolerable. They still were incarcerated, but they ate better. A radio was provided for the dormitory, and the one thin cotton blanket that was supposed to keep them warm at night was replaced by a thicker wool one.

There was much to be learned at the school. The boys were taught to lie, to cheat, and to steal, mostly by the older residents. There were supervised days outside the compound, about one a year. That was when the boys practiced what they had learned. They stole food from grocery stores and fruit stands. They were perfect little liars when they were caught.

The boys broke up into groups, or gangs. It was the best way to stay safe. Charles was the youngest of five Indian boys that hung around together. The oldest, a Seminole, was fifteen and almost a hardened criminal. He was strong, and had fashioned a knife from a spoon. He kept the other boys from danger, but they also learned to be bitter, and to be wary of the white boys who only wanted to do them harm.

Charles had a few fist fights over the next few years, and he was cut slightly once, but he survived. He started plotting his escape when he was ten, and shortly after his twelfth birthday, made good on his plan. It was 1916.

Chapter Seventeen

Charles, now called Charlie on the streets of Richmond, would not have lasted long were it not for an intervention. He had tracked down the address of the Amundsens, but they'd moved. None of the neighbors knew where the couple had gone.

At the age of twelve, there was only one avenue by which to survive in the world of the homeless, and Charlie took it. He used the cover of darkness to find food and drink. He did not discriminate. Any store that he could break into was fair game in his desperate mind.

He had lived two weeks in a makeshift encampment in a densely wooded area just outside of town, using stolen blankets and a tent made of canvas he had stolen from a general store. His food supply was running low so he ventured into town shortly before midnight on a moonlit night to forage for anything he could eat.

Charlie had no way of knowing that the Richmond City Council had hired a security guard in the wake of so many break-ins. They picked an off-duty policeman who was working, patrolling by bicycle on the night the boy showed up looking for an easy target. They didn't encounter each other until Charlie was leaving a store, his loot in a knapsack slung over one shoulder.

The cop was a rather large individual, and Charlie was just average for a twelve-year old. He had not yet developed a man's body. It was no contest as the guard overpowered the desperate boy.

"Let me loose," shouted the Indian boy, with fear showing in his squeaky voice.

It was only then that the guard realized he had captured a mere child. "I'm afraid I can't do that, son." He said. "You ought to know better than to steal. I'm taking you home to your folks."

"I ain't got no folks." Charlie blurted, impulsively. He immediately regretted saying it, fearing he would be sent back to the home from which he had escaped.

"What do you mean? Where do you live?" Charlie's captor questioned loudly. There was no answer.

The off-duty policeman, Andrew Dark, was married and had two children, twins, a boy and a girl. This wayward youth in front of him looked to be just a little older.

"What's your name boy?" The older man had softened his tone.

"I ain't saying." Charlie answered, fearful of being tracked back to the boy's home.

"Well, I guess you leave me no choice but to turn you in, and put you in the juvenile delinquent system." That would be the easy option.

"It's Charlie, Charlie Redbird." The boy muttered, feeling that his only chance of not being sent back, was to come clean to this stranger, who held his life in his hands.

"That's better. Now we're getting somewhere." Dark said. "Where are you staying?"

"I have a camp in the woods. It's not far out of town." Charlie answered, more forthcoming now.

Andrew Dark made a decision on that dimly lit city street that would have far-reaching consequences, though he didn't know it then. He took the wayward youth he had caught to his home, rather than the police station. He didn't write it up. He didn't report it at all. He could see his own son in the eyes of Charlie Redbird, and he hoped that his boy would be protected by some stranger too, in this kind of situation.

Andrew's wife Rosemary was as compassionate as her husband. She had wanted another child, although not a twelve-year old one, and not an Indian, though there wasn't a prejudiced bone in her body. It would be a sacrifice. But the alternative was not a good one. She couldn't stand the thought of putting this child into the State's system. She felt, justifiably, that he would be ruined for life.

So it was that the twelve-year old Cherokee Indian Charlie Redbird came to live with the family of policeman Andrew Dark and his wife Rosemary, and became, in effect, their third child. Coincidentally the Richmond crime wave became a thing of the past.

Chapter Eighteen

The next few years were not easy for Andrew Dark or his family. The Great War was unfolding in Europe, and when the United States was pulled into it, Andrew was drafted into the Army. He could have gotten a deferment, but Andrew was, to say the least, an honorable man.

The red-headed second generation Irishman had joined the police force to do good, not for the glory, or the steady work. He had little education, as his parents had been poor, and had no means to transport their children, of which there were five, to school, let alone provide them with decent clothes. His father had worked in the mines of West Virginia before a cave-in claimed his life. His mother took in washing to feed them.

Andrew was sent overseas almost immediately. Rosemary and the children were left to cope with less money for necessities, but they managed.

Charlie was enrolled in school with the Dark children. He worried that the authorities would find him and send him back to the place from which he had escaped. What he didn't know was that the new headmaster of the institution didn't report him missing. Had he done that, he would have lost some of his funding, since the money from the State was tied to the number of boys incarcerated there. He was a thoroughly dishonest individual, and had gotten away with his schemes so far.

The three children became close over the next few years. Early on, Rosemary would read Andrew's letters to them. Of course the soldier didn't tell his family of the horrors of war, only that he was safe, and missed them terribly. When he returned without a scratch, and with a chest full of medals, they were proud and excited. Life could once again return to normal.

The children of the South had been told over and over by their church-going parents that the minorities of the United States were less than human, and deserved no respect or consideration. Lincoln had been a traitor to his country when he freed the slaves. Indians and Mexicans were not much, if any, better. Most of the kids bought it, and treated people of color accordingly. Andrew and Rosemary Dark were the exception. They felt that all people were God's children and deserved to be respected equally.

Charlie was ridiculed at school in the beginning for being an inferior Indian. Jonathon, Andrew's son, stood up for his friend, and roommate. Often he would go home with a black-eye and skinned knees for his trouble. Later, as Charlie outgrew most of the boys at school, he didn't need protection. They didn't like him, but they were afraid, and left him alone.

Eileen Dark was a skinny, but cute little blonde as a twelve-year old. Her brother and Charlie didn't have much time for her. When they would go off in the woods chasing squirrels and rabbits, she stayed home helping her mother with the housework. As the years went by, that changed. Eileen grew into a very attractive teen-ager. Her body was almost fully developed by the time she reached fourteen.

Soon Charlie and his blood-brother Jonathon became aware of Eileen and her charm. She was no longer to be avoided. Jonathon was proud and protective of his sister, while Charlie didn't understand the hormones of his developing body. He fought off the urges he felt when he was near Eileen.

By 1919 Charlie and the two Dark kids were going to the cinema quite often. They were able to see The Birth of a Nation, which was still playing in Southern theaters. Jonathon liked Mary Pickford films. Charlie just tagged along to be near Eileen. He didn't dare sit next to her in the movies, though. Her brother sat between them. He did steal glances at her whenever he thought no one would see.

It was inevitable that there would come a time when the two kids were alone in the house. It was the day before Eileen's eighteenth birthday. They both had graduated that June, and Andrew's daughter was spending the Summer at home before heading off to college. In that day very few women went on to higher learning, so everyone was very proud of her. There was to be a party the next day, not only to celebrate her birthday, but also to acknowledge her achievement.

On the day before the big event Eileen's father was at work, while Rosemary hurried about shopping for the party. Jonathon was job hunting. He wanted no part of the white-collar world. He wanted to work with his hands.

Charlie was in the kitchen looking for something to feed his huge body, and Eileen was in her bedroom, primping. She was fully aware of the effect she was having on the big Indian boy, and she decided it was time to do something about it. She called to him that she needed help finding something. Obediently he came to her open door. She stood by her bed, wearing only a white brassiere and bloomers. She walked over to where he stood, his mouth agape. She reached for his hand

"Touch them." She said, softly, pulling his big paw up until he cupped one breast. He didn't squeeze, he didn't move his fingers looking for a nipple. He was as inexperienced as she. He said nothing.

Eileen released the hand that she had covered so as to place both hands on his large leather belt, loosening it. As she began unbuttoning his trousers he should have heard the bell ringing in his head, telling him to stop, that this was wrong. He heard nothing. It was all feeling at this point. He was fully aroused, and, though he might have wished to, he couldn't hide it.

She was doing the things that the girls at school had talked about. Some were experienced, others were engaging in fantasy. She moved her hands away from him, reaching behind her to unfasten the garment that was holding her breasts. When the brassiere fell to the linoleum floor Charlie could do nothing but stare. They were quickly arriving at the point of no return.

He felt he should be doing something to show that he knew what was going on, that he was the man. He reached behind her head, pulling her lips to his. She quickly opened her mouth slightly, and moved her tongue over his lips. This was designed to excite him more. It worked. He pressed his body fully upon hers. She moved her hips back and forth slowly, teasing him.

Charlie blurted, "I love you, Eileen."

She smiled, and reached for his pants again unbuttoning them. As they fell she could see his arousal, and quickly pulled his underpants down around his knees.

He groped at her bloomers, and was able to disengage them from her hips, so that she too was completely exposed. He spoke softly this time. "God, you're beautiful."

They quickly moved to her bed. She laid back and he fell on her. She spread her slim white legs obligingly, guiding him into her. She screamed softly, more like a loud moan, as his manhood tore her hymen.

Rosemary had realized that she needed her list, and she had left it on the kitchen counter at home. As she entered the front room she heard her daughter scream. Thinking the girl might be hurt she rushed into Eileen's bedroom. Seeing the two youngsters coupled on the bed was almost too much for her. Her knees buckled and she nearly fell. "Oh my God!" She screamed. "What are you doing?"

Charlie quickly disengaged himself and, trying to hide by covering his genitals with his hands, he found his shorts on the floor, and ran out of the room, leaving his pants. Eileen didn't move, but covered herself with her blanket. Her face was beet red.

Rosemary went to the kitchen, picked up the phone and dialed the operator. Instead of asking for her husband she said, "get me the police!"

Charles Redbird was charged and convicted of rape of a minor, since he was eighteen and she was still only seventeen. He was sentenced to four years in the state penitentiary. The four years became seven as he engaged in numerous fights in prison. In the last one he gave his white assailant a concussion. He was released in September of 1929

Andrew had gotten the truth from his daughter finally, after her conscience got the better of her. She was all right, after all. There had been no permanent harm to her. He loved Eileen, but as a man he understood what had happened.

During the time that Charlie Redbird was in prison, Jonathon applied and was accepted as an apprentice fireman for the city of Richmond.

Eileen went away to college. While there she met and married a doctor. She quit school. Their attempts at conceiving a child were fruitless. She became depressed, and one dreary day while her husband was away, she slit her wrists. She bled out before anyone found her.

Andrew Dark had intended to meet Charlie at the prison gate when he was released but he was tied up by a case. He still wasn't ready to give up on Charlie. As it turned out, the policeman arrived at the prison an hour after Charlie was released and the Indian was gone. They never saw each other again.

Chapter Nineteen

It was still early when I brought Rachel back to her house after dinner. She had turned the radio on, found a top ten music show, and we sat on her couch just listening to the soft sounds of Jo Stafford and others.

I realized something, sitting there with her, that I had not really thought of in years. My personal life was a wreck. I'd been so wrapped up in making myself worthy of Annie, that everything else took a back seat. I was chasing a fantasy that had its roots in a time when I was too young to know what life was all about. Even the war didn't change my outlook. I'm not saying there weren't a few women. I'm not a monk. They just went along with the drinking I did in consolation for screwing it up with Annie. Now here was a woman sitting next to me that made me think I might have a chance at a life after all.

She interrupted my train of thought. "Do you dance Ivan?"

"Not hardly," I answered. "My left foot doesn't pay attention to my right one, and neither one is connected to my brain. Other than that I have no problem with it."

She laughed. It was a good laugh. Not phony. Not giggly like a teen-ager. "I think you're good for me," she sounded sincere. "but I still want to dance." She stood up and reached her free arm out to me. When I got up in response, she quickly shed the sling that was holding her other arm in place.

"Are you sure you want to do that?" I questioned.

"It doesn't hurt now."

"I hope it stays that way. I'd rather be helping you than hurting." I meant it.

We danced in an area away from her throw rug, more toward the kitchen. She moved easily, and I was better than I'd implied. We weren't cheek to cheek, but I was enjoying it. The song was a Tony Martin ballad. "Is your shoulder okay?" I asked.

"It's fine. I said you are good for me."

I took a chance, and kissed her on her lips. She didn't seem to respond, and I thought I had misread her. She pulled away gently, and said, "There's something I need to show you."

She left me and went into the bedroom. Presently she returned with a piece of paper in her right hand. "I lied to you before. I didn't know if I could trust you, and I was afraid."

126

She handed me an envelope. "What am I supposed to do with this?" I asked.

"It was from Phillip. I did receive one letter from him. Look at the postmark." She stated dramatically.

The mark was pretty faint, but I could make out where it came from-Nacogdoches, Texas. "How long have you had this?" I asked, all thought of romance gone for the moment.

"He sent it not long after he left me. You can read the letter if you like." Her look and tone gave me the impression that she really didn't want me to.

"No. It's personal. I don't really need to see it." I doubted there was anything in the letter that would help me anyway. But now I had a place to go. I'd been pretty much at a dead-end.

I continued, "Thanks Rachel. I know it took a lot for you to show me this." I held the envelope up.

She had a concerned look on her face. "There's something else. I should have told you sooner."

"What do you mean?" I asked.

She stepped closer and took my hand. "I don't think the killer was shooting at you the other day!"

"We've been through this. Why would you think that?" I was confused.

127

Rachel spoke again, slowly and softly, still holding my hand, and looking into my eyes, as if searching for a reaction. "It happened a few months ago. A man came to my house to ask me for a date. I refused, and he was angered. He grabbed me and forced me into my bedroom," She paused, still looking in my eyes, "where he raped me!"

I was stunned. I reached out to hold her, but she pushed me away.

"Can't you see? I'm damaged goods." Tears came to her eyes as she moved to a chair and slumped down.

"Who was the bastard? Do you know his name?" All I could think of was finding this coward, and killing him.

She could see the fury in my eyes. "Yes. But I don't know if I should tell you. You can't go after him. He threatened me that if I went to the police, he would return and kill me. I felt that he really meant it."

"Give me his name, and I will take care of it where he'll never bother you again." But silently I was afraid that all the evidence would have long since disappeared, and it would be that piece of crap's word against hers. But the attempted murder was something else. I was sure we could make that rap stick.

Suddenly it all made sense. When I came to town asking questions, This crud must have followed me, thinking that when I went to see Rachel, she was going to tell me about the rape and give him up. I repeated myself, forcefully, "Who is he?"

"His name is Harold Lambright. He works at the newspaper office." She seemed relieved to finally get it out in the open. She'd been keeping the terror she must have felt hidden for a long time.

"He was the guy who gave me a lift to the rental car agency. He probably waited and followed me from there to your place. I thought he was doing me a favor." It also occurred to me that he would have access to a rifle from his parent's place. Hell, maybe they were even in on it. "How could I have been so dumb?" I said aloud.

"You didn't know." She answered.

Suddenly I had to get out of there. I wanted to put the wheels in motion to put the younger Lambright behind bars for a long time. "Is there someone who can come and stay with you until I get back? I need to see the cop Andrew Dark."

She answered, "My son will be home in a couple of days. Can't you call the police, and stay with me until then?"

I was anxious to see this resolved, but she made sense. At least they could pick the guy up, and get him off the streets for a while. By then the soldier would be home to help protect his mother, while I helped wrap up the evidence to send Lambright away for a long time.

I called the police station, and presently Dark came on the line. I laid the whole thing out for him, and he was going to check it out with the city attorney but agreed that there was probably enough information to arrest Harold Lambright, and hold him for questioning.

Rachel was exhausted. It had been a stressful day. She found me some blankets, and excused herself. I remembered the feeling I had had when we came back to her place, so I sat up in vigilance for most of the night. I finally fell asleep around three.

Chapter Twenty

With Harold Lambright safely tucked away in a cell, and bail set high enough to likely keep him there, I turned my eyes on Texas. I would rather have concentrated on Rachel, but she just wasn't ready. We both knew it.

Thomas Embree arrived home on schedule, which was a relief to his mother. He seemed like a nice kid. I wouldn't have expected less, him being kin to Rachel. Anyway that freed me from guard duty, so that I could get on with the work I was being paid for.

I would have had to fly to Dallas, rent a car, and then drive back to Nacogdoches, and it seemed like backtracking to me, so I bought a bus ticket. I would only have to change once, and the route would be pretty direct. I left on a Wednesday, just two days after Rachel was discharged from the hospital.

I had a lot of time to think during that bumpy bus ride. I didn't get much sleep that night. I was pretty sure that, in time, the German Luger pistol found in West Virginia would be traced back to the elder Lambright's gun collection, just as the rifle would be.

Wouldn't it be too bad if it was determined that John Lambright, Rodney's father, had brought the pistol to the bank that day, and had fired the fatal shot that killed Phillip Atchison the second. Carrying it a step farther, the insurance company that had paid out the fortune on which Rodney and Louise were living, could well void the insurance and force the couple to pay it back, possibly bankrupting them. I remember thinking it couldn't happen to two nicer people.

The authorities never actually placed Phillip the Third at the bank, so he was basically in the clear. Of course he wouldn't know that, and would think himself a fugitive still.

Rachel had definitely been scarred by the rape. It would take time for her to really trust any man enough to let him touch her, let alone to allow him into her bed. It would probably require a gentleness that most of the male species didn't possess. I would like to be the one to try, though. She really got to me. It would be far too premature to say I was in love with her, but that's the way I felt.

Now to the work ahead. Phillip Atchison the Third would most certainly have changed his name, thinking he was a fugitive. That would complicate the search immensely. All I had to go on was an old picture of him as a young teen-ager in cowboy garb. His ten-gallon hat even hid some of his facial features. Rachel had given me a general description, but I was sure that my search would require a great amount of legwork and interviews with the townsfolk of Nacogdoches.

When the big Greyhound bus crossed from Louisiana into Texas it occurred to me that a small town like the one to which I was headed, might not even have a car rental agency. Great time to think of it.

As we pulled into Nacogdoches I was surprised. The place was bigger than I thought it would be. I had believed the smell of oil and cattle would be in the air but I was mistaken. There were oil wells visible just outside of the city, and fences that, I was sure held cattle at bay, but the town had a clean smell, almost like magnolias. Another misconception I had was disproved when I saw the modern buildings along the main street. I'd been sure it would be like the old west, maybe even with horse troughs and hitching posts.

After renting a car, I found a modest hotel room downtown. I didn't want to blow all my expense account on nice amenities. Hopefully I wouldn't be in town long anyway. It occurred to me that I would be really conspicuous in this western town with my Chicago clothes, so the next thing I did was go shopping, which was way down on my list of things I liked to do. I didn't go so far as to buy a big hat. I thought it would just make my head look smaller.

It made sense that the people in town most likely to be able to help me find Phillip Atchison, in addition to older people, would be either a barber who loved to gossip, or a waitress, who seemed to know everyone. It used to be that, in small western towns, there were always old guys sitting around outside passing time reminiscing about the old days. Maybe that would still be true in Nacogdoches.

I hadn't eaten since Mississippi, so I decided to go the waitress route first. The sign out front advertised GREAT EATS in huge letters, and I decided to let them prove it. I found a booth in a corner and waited. Soon a skinny thing about twenty, dressed in white, with a chef's hat, and wearing an apron, approached me. All of a sudden I was having second thoughts. Anyone that slim probably didn't even dine at Great Eats. Or the food wasn't good enough to eat a lot of. I've always felt more comfortable with wide-bodied waitresses.

"What can I get you, stranger?" Her voice and her smile seemed right friendly as she handed me a menu that consisted of one sheet of paper.

"How about a cup of coffee while I look this thing over?" I held out the menu, and flashed her my best smile.

"Sure thing," she answered. "You just take all the time you want." And away she went.

I decided on a country fried steak and waved to the little thing in the apron, who was sitting on a counter stool not too far away. She jumped to her feet and quickly shuffled over to my table with the same smile as before. I gave her my order and waited.

After a so-so lunch, and when the girl brought my check, I hauled out the picture of Phillip. She said he didn't look familiar, and she would remember if he did, because he was so good-looking and all. I thanked her, left a buck on the table, and followed her up to the cash register.

Asking the barber didn't turn out to be such a good idea either. He was old enough, but didn't remember seeing the boy in the picture. He did say that if Phillip was a cowboy, it would explain why he hadn't seen him. Most of the ranch hands cut their own hair. When they did come to town it was to find a woman or a bottle, or both. So the old west was alive after all.

I spent the rest of the day wandering about town talking to any local who would give me the time of day. That would be about half of them.

When my feet began to hurt I headed back to the hotel. A hot bath sounded good about then. It was about eight that night when I heard a knock on my door. I was suspicious, considering what happened at the hotel in Richmond when I had an unsolicited visitor. At this place there was no peephole, so I would just have to take my chances.

When I opened the door I was surprised to see a woman standing outside. She looked to be about thirty-five. She stood only about five feet, and I had the feeling she had once been pretty. But the years had taken that away somehow, and she seemed a little dowdy, even doleful. The corners of her mouth were turned downward, and her clothes were old and wrinkled. There was a dullness to her brown eyes, and her hair, which was the same color, was uncombed.

When she spoke, her voice had a gravelly quality to it, not at all like the high-pitched tone of most of the females I knew. "Are y'all the one lookin' for my fiancé?

Chapter Twenty-One

I was beginning to feel like I was looking for a cork in the ocean. I knew where it was thrown in, and the current had led me to this small Texas town. It had bobbed up briefly, but then it was gone again, and I had no idea in which direction. I even thought maybe it had lost its buoyancy and sunk, never to surface again. Now this waif of a woman had shown up on my doorstep, so to speak, perhaps with a map that would lead me to my treasure.

"I'm looking for Phillip Atchison the third, if that's who you mean?" I would have crossed my fingers and toes if that would bring me the answer I was hoping for.

"Do you mind if I sit down? I'm awful tired." She said, looking around for a place to light.

"I'm sorry. There's a chair in the corner." I said, pointing. She did look beat.

After slouching in the one chair in the room, she continued, "I don't know any Phillip whatever you said, but your description sounds like the man I was supposed to marry, until he hightailed it out of town."

My heart skipped a beat. I thought maybe I was getting close, but now it seemed like just another dead-end. "So he's not here anymore? Is that what you're telling me?"

"That's right, stranger," she answered, flippantly. "You got anything to drink? I sure am dry." She changed the subject.

"Only tap water. Sorry." Right then I wished I had a fifth of bourbon. Maybe that would loosen her tongue. But I couldn't chance leaving her before I learned what she knew. "How do you know that the man I'm searching for is your guy?"

I held my breath as she answered, "I have the same picture you been flashing all over town."

I was impressed, "Tell me about him. To begin with, what name do you know him by?" I was becoming excited. It had to be the same person.

"His name's Jeb Lee. I met him not long after he came to Nacogdoches. It was 1930. I was only sixteen. He was a cowhand working at my father's ranch, the Double R."

I sat down on the sagging bed facing her as she continued, "He took to the cowboy life right away. It was as if he had been born into it." Her eyes lit up as she remembered.

"At first he didn't even notice me, but I was interested right away. I never got to town, and didn't know any boys. I was starting to feel like a woman, if you know what I mean?" I nodded in the affirmative. At least I thought I did.

"We kept bumping into each other on the ranch, when I was out riding and such. One night about a year later, when my father was at a cattleman's meeting, I invited him to my room. After that, he snuck in every chance he got."

"Where was your mother while this was going on?" I was curious.

"She had died from consumption a few years earlier."

"Why did he leave?"

She looked thoughtful, "He had a friend, an Indian. One day a travelling man came to town from out west. He told them both that there was work in Hollywood for stunt men. The pay was better than here, and the work easier, if they didn't mind a few bumps and bruises. The Indian, I think his name was Charlie, was having trouble with the foreman on the oil rig he was working the other side of the county, so he was ready to pick up and leave for greener pastures. He talked my man into going along. Jeb swore he would send for me when he got settled in California, But he never did."

I thought I saw a tear in her eye as she finished. "Do you think he's still there?" I asked.

"I don't know." She looked wistful. "The last time I heard from him was the day he left."

"You've been very helpful Miss, I'm sorry, I don't even know your name."

"It's Celia, Celia Devin." She replied.

"I'm Ivan Dunn, Celia. It's nice to meet you. If I catch up with him, what would you like me to tell him?"

She looked thoughtful, then she answered, "Tell him I still love him."

"After all these years? Are you sure that's what you want?" I felt sorry for her. Time had not been good to this woman who sat across from me.

"You're probably right. It's too late for us." She rose, and taking my hand, said, "Good luck Mister Dunn. If you ever get back this way, stop by and let me know if you found Jeb."

"Are you still out at the ranch?" I asked.

"No, I haven't been out there since my father died a few years back. I lost the ranch to creditors. I work at the Right Way Saloon now, and bunk upstairs."

That would explain her forlorn looks. "I'll be sure to let you know if I locate him. Maybe I will send a letter." I knew I would make a special effort. This girl didn't need any more heartache. I made sure to get her official address before she left.

I caught the train for Los Angeles the next morning.

Chapter Twenty-Two

As the train pulled into Union Station just before dark on a clear but windy Sunday evening, I had the feeling I was getting close to wrapping up my investigation, and I was ready. It had been a frustrating case. At first I was sympathetic for the kid who had lost everything that day at the bank. I could almost feel his pain when he had to leave his girl, and embark on a journey into oblivion. Hell, he was just a child. But then I met Celia Devin. He hadn't been honest with her. He had used her for his own gratification, lying about his intentions. I was sure he never intended to marry the girl. He took everything she had to give, and never looked back. So now my outlook had changed considerably, and I just wanted to end the hunt, but not before finding Phillip/Jeb and giving him a piece of my mind.

Most of the movie studios were in the San Fernando Valley, so after renting yet another car I headed out that way to find a place to stay, for what I hoped would be only one night.

I found a set of cabins in the Burbank area and settled into one of them for the night.

The next day about ten I headed out to find the Republic lot. They were making most of the westerns, and I deduced that genre would be the one to use stunt men more than any other. I was stopped at the gate by a security guard. I told him my reason for being there in as short a form as I could. I was informed politely that I couldn't be allowed access to the lot because I didn't have a pass, and I wasn't on the list to be admitted. I had anticipated this, and had a story ready that, if it didn't bring tears to the guard's eyes, it would at least get me in. I told him that Jeb Lee's mother was dying, and I, his brother had been entrusted to bring the news to her other son.

The guard was impressed with my eloquence, and though I'm not sure he bought it, and he still didn't let me enter, he did confide to me at which bar the stunt people hung out. I thanked him profusely as I left, wiping the tears from my eyes.

It wasn't hard to find the place the guard had told me about. When I walked into the dimly lit bar, and my eyes became accustomed to the setting, I noticed that it was almost empty. Of course it was only eleven something in the morning. There was one woman at a table near the entrance, and two men at the bar who were not sitting together. None were in cowboy garb. I didn't hold out much hope that I would learn anything, but since I was already there, I went up to the bar and sat strategically between the two gentlemen. I assumed that if I asked the bartender the million-dollar question the other two would hear me, and that way I wouldn't have to repeat it.

I ordered a manhattan, and when the bartender brought it I casually asked if any stuntmen usually came in after work. He replied in the affirmative, and helpfully added that they usually began showing up at five-thirty. I was encouraged so much that I downed my drink and ordered another while he was still across from me. This next one I would be sure to sip lest I forget why I was there in the first place. Since none of the other patrons provided any further information, I left after finishing my drink.

After polishing off two stiff drinks there was no way I was getting behind the wheel of the rental car, so I started walking around the area where the bar was located. I had over four hours to kill. I found a theater that was showing a double-feature, only a few blocks from the bar. I settled in to watch a John Wayne war movie, The Sands of Iwo Jima. By the time the second show started I was fast asleep. I awoke sometime in the middle of the second showing of the one I had already seen. It was six o'clock.

I wandered over to the bar, trying hard to conceal the excitement I felt for the fact that my search might finally be over. I pictured in my mind the scene when Phillip and I finally met. They say there are two sides to every story, and the one I knew was definitely not favorable to my quarry. Still, I was interested in what he would have to say. He probably wouldn't even know I was looking for him. He would however, think he was being pursued by the authorities from Virginia, and maybe even the FBI. I would have to watch myself so as to not spook him into running.

I knew that when I opened the door to the place, I wouldn't be able to see much for a few minutes, as dark as they kept it in there. As soon as I stepped in I could hear the buzz of conversation that told me there were lots of customers. Let's hope my guy is one of them, I said to myself. As the silhouettes began to take shape, I stepped up to the bar. The same bartender from before was on duty.

"What can I get you sir?" He was cordial.

"I'll have a manhattan." The buzz from the earlier drinks had worn off during my nap.

"Sure thing. You're the guy who was in earlier." He observed.

"That's right. I'm looking for a stunt man by the name of Jeb Lee." I began, "I'm not sure if he works on the Republic lot, though. I'm just looking for a little help locating him."

"I'll ask around. I don't know him myself." With that he walked out onto the crowded floor where the tables were located. I watched him as he moved from one table to another.

My eyesight was improving, and I could see quite a few men dressed in cowboy garb from days gone by. There were even some women mixed in.

When the bartender moved back behind the bar he didn't come over right away. He was mixing drinks and getting beers for his steady customers. After delivering all the booze, he stopped by where I was sitting.

"Nobody here seems to know the man you asked about. There aren't many western movies being made these days. Are you sure this Jeb Lee is a cowboy stunt man?" He was trying to be helpful.

"No I'm not," I answered, "and I'm not positive he's even still in town. I lost track of him when we both were kids. I guess I'm just clutching at straws, as the saying goes."

"Well I wish you luck." He said as he walked away.

It was dark when I drove back to my hotel room. I needed to reevaluate where I was going with my search. Every lead I had turned out to be a dead-end. I couldn't seem to bridge the twenty years since Phillip left Rachel, and disappeared into that Richmond night. I thought I was close a couple of times, only to realize I was not even in the right State. I needed a new approach. But what? I still hadn't come up with an answer when I fell asleep.

An idea came to me in the middle of the night. I awoke to find myself sideways on the bed, with most of my covers on the floor. I didn't remember dreaming, but I must have thrashed around some. The reason nobody remembered seeing Jeb or Phillip, besides the time element, was that he was ordinary. He didn't look out of place. Even though someone I talked to might have seen him, they wouldn't remember. I knew he was travelling with an Indian, and I even had a name-Charlie. Most of the stuntmen, even the ones playing Indians were white, with a ton of makeup. A real Indian would stand out. It was so simple, I was surprised I hadn't thought of it before.

The stereotypical native couldn't handle his liquor, and might have ended up in trouble because of it. I made a mental note to check with the local police, maybe even the jail. If that approach didn't bear fruit, I could go back to the bar near the studio. Republic wasn't the only movie-maker in town. There were others where Jeb and Charlie might have worked. It would be easier if I knew the Indian's last name. I might check out newspaper reports at the library, too. Who knows? I was due for a little luck. I felt better as I fell asleep for the second time that night.

Chapter Twenty-Three

Ruth Emerson was not born in Reno, Nevada. When she was growing up in a little New Hampshire town she never imagined she would end up in that rowdy hamlet out west with the huge sign, THE BIGGEST LITTLE CITY IN THE WORLD hanging over Virginia Street.

Ruth, a precocious sixteen year old, was almost full-grown when her mother packed her up and sent her by train to earn her keep with her Aunt Adele Martin. Addie, as she was affectionately referred to, ran a boarding house in Reno, and Ruth would be able to earn her keep as a housemaid, freeing the spinster Adele to spend more time in the gaming establishments downtown.

By the time the transplanted New England girl met the flamboyant Jeb Lee in 1933 she had given birth to two girls out of wedlock. The first was the product of a rape and taken from her by her aunt, who had no children of her own, under the pretense that Ruth was too young to raise a child, with no husband to help. Ruth would become the aunt, and Adele the mother to the baby that Adele named Marie. The poor girl had no choice but to agree, since the elder woman provided what little livelihood she had. The second child, born in 1932, was hidden from Adele and adopted out of Oakland, California, where Ruth had fled to a Salvation Army home when she began to show signs of the pregnancy. The father, whom she had thought would save her from her fate, had left for parts unknown when he found out his paramour was with child.

Ruth was a cute, curly-headed, brown-haired girl with a slim body, and full breasts. She tanned easily. After each birth she regained her figure quickly, and her bosom seemed to gain volume, which made her more attractive to the men of Reno who had occasion to stay at her aunt's house.

Had the shy waif from New Hampshire had more self-esteem, the degrading events that befell her may not have occurred. When the rodeo cowboy happened into her life, she was extremely vulnerable. He was also a tenant of her aunt's.

Jeb was very self-assured by that time. He had become really good with horses from his time in Texas, and he had learned some rope tricks in his spare time. He had reluctantly left the ranch in Nacogdoches to become a stunt man, and he was even less sure about Reno.

Charlie, his only friend, had become persona non-gratis at the oil fields of the northeastern Texas town, because of a fight he had with the boss. It was not of his doing, but just the same he had to pay the consequences. The man in charge had ended up in the hospital with a broken jaw and a few cracked ribs. Fortunately Charlie had the offer from the stuntman's agent just before the incident that got him fired. He convinced Jeb to go with him, and they both had found work in Hollywood.

The pilgrimage to Reno was yet another case of Jeb's friend's whim. When the studio became disenchanted with the real Indian, and Charlie decided to try the rodeo life, Jeb figured what the hell, he couldn't get any more torn up than was the case in Hollywood. Any time now he could be seriously injured with the ever increasing difficulty of the stunts. The last time, he had almost been run over by the wheels of the stagecoach when he'd been asked to fall off a lead horse after feigning being shot, then falling under the vehicle. He accomplished the trick, but not until the third take. He spent many hours in a hot bath after that one. As it turned out both Jeb and Charlie took up residence at the boarding house of Adele Martin.

Ruth was becoming enamored of the charismatic rodeo star. They spent many hours together in the evenings, just the two of them, up in the nearby hills west of town. They would spread a blanket out in a clearing, lay back and try to make out the constellations in the vast clear sky.

With Jeb it was different. He was gentle, not rushing her. She truly felt she was in love with him, and had no doubt they would be married. The young cowboy was very fond of Ruth, but to say he was in love would not be true. In fact he had a similar relationship with another woman at the same time.

It seemed as if any semblance of conscience had left Jeb Lee about the time of the ill-fated train ride from Virginia. There was no trace of the child who had witnessed his father being gunned down in the Richmond bank. When he met a shy girl from a prominent banking family in town, he was already involved with Ruth Emerson. He didn't know it at the time but the fertile housemaid was once again with child.

It was ironic that Margaret Lincoln's father was the president of the Washoe County Bank. Jeb met the older man when he applied for a loan to purchase a house. Margaret happened to be visiting the bank at the time, and was introduced to the bank's prospective customer.

Jarod Lincoln loved his daughter, but she was almost twenty-three with no possible husband on the horizon. Most girls were married by that time in their lives, and had children. Her father did not relish the idea of his only girl growing old as a spinster. There was also a financial consideration, since he did not want to continue being her benefactor all her life.

Jeb was young, apparently healthy, and reasonably good-looking. The rodeo cowboy had at least a temporary job. Therefore he was qualified to be a suitor to his daughter. When the young man showed an interest in Margaret, and she in him, Jarod Lincoln pounced. He offered Jeb, not only the home loan, but also to set him up in business if they did in fact get married.

As Ruth Emerson began to show signs of her condition, Jeb was forced to confront his dilemma. He had decided that his future would be secure with his marriage to Margaret Lincoln, and he couldn't pass that up for a poor housemaid and her offspring, no matter how attractive the girl was.

When he told her of his decision, Ruth was heart-broken. She loved him so. He was the first man she had ever felt so strongly for. In order to temper the blow Jeb offered to pay the expense of an abortion. She would not agree. It would be murder-the death of a part of her. The thought was so abhorrent to her that she fled from him, and when the time came for her child to be born, she entered a maternity home, and delivered her first boy.

Ruth used her mother's maiden name at the home so as to hide the birth from her aunt. Instead of being born Edward Emerson, the baby was given the name Edward Fenton. When the owner of the maternity home, Alice Jones, realized how destitute the mother was, she arranged an adoption, and kept Ruth on to work for her when she recovered. The only payment received by the kindly Alice was that the child was given the middle name of Jones.

Meanwhile, Jeb Lee married Margaret Lincoln, with Charlie Redbird serving as a reluctant best man. He really liked Ruth, and felt sorry for her. Charlie was the only one to visit the lonely girl in the hospital. It was on her twenty-first birthday, two days after Edward was born.

Though the child didn't know it, he was very fortunate to be adopted by not only a loving couple, but one that was equipped to care for and provide a home as he grew to manhood. That was not an easy feat in 1934 during the depression.

After a few months Alice received a picture of Edward from his new parents. She immediately gave it to Ruth, who was still working at the home. Many years later, mother and son would be reunited, and he would show her the same picture that she had carried with her and protected for all that time.

The rodeo and its performers prospered during the rest of the thirties, while world unrest deepened. Jeb's shop did well, and Ruth finally found a man who would love and care for her. She remained in Reno until 1937, never seeing Jeb. Charlie even stopped coming by when she met the man who would become her husband. After they were married they relocated to Stockton, California. Within a year Ruth delivered a baby girl. She would keep this child, and the two other girls that were to come later.

Chapter Twenty-Four

I first noticed the guy in the bar by the movie studio. He didn't fit the scenario. He was wearing a print shirt, like he just got back from Hawaii. He had on baggy brown slacks that looked as if he got them from a fat man. They were pinched at the belt, and made him look sloppy. He wasn't very tall, maybe five-five. I didn't get a good look at his face, but his hair was very dark. He could have been Mexican for all I knew. I would have thought he was tailing someone else, but for the fact that he left the bar right after me.

The next day I spotted him again when I went out for breakfast. He was across the street reading what looked like a newspaper. Who does that on the sidewalk? At the restaurant I asked my usual questions. I was sitting at the counter, and the guy next to me was just having coffee. So I struck up a conversation.

"Do you live around here?" I began.

He smiled as he turned to face me. "No. I work at Republic, but I live further out the Valley."

"I've been looking for a stunt man. I don't know if he's at your studio or not. Nobody seems to have seen him."

He was thoughtful, "What's his name?"

"Jeb Lee. He came from East Texas, but he may not have been here long."

"That name doesn't ring a bell. Did you try the bar around the block? A lot of the stunt men hang out there." He was trying to be helpful.

"Yes. I've been there. No one seems to know him." I answered, "but the problem is that he might not be here anymore. I lost track of him in 1931."

"And you really expect to find him now?" He was incredulous.

"I know it's a long shot, but it's pretty important that I locate him. He has a lot of money coming." I lied. And then I remembered that I had an alternative lead. "How about an Indian named Charlie? He was a stuntman too, and I heard they were pals."

"No that name doesn't ring a bell either." He answered, "but have you tried other studios?" He was really trying to be helpful.

"Not yet. But it looks like my next step. Any suggestions on which one I should start with?" I was hopeful he would come up with something useful.

"You know, I do have an idea, but it's a long shot."

"That's all I've had so far. What's your opinion?" I was groping for anything.

He looked down at his meal as he framed his words. "About the time your man disappeared, there was a new movie studio in town. It was started by a Judge. He called it Magistrate Movies. They didn't last long. The competition was too tough from the big guys, but they made a few westerns before the roof caved in."

"Are any of them still around?" I asked, hopefully.

"A few. They would have been picked up by the other studios because of their experience." He said, "Why don't you check at the hiring hall over on Sunset?"

I cursed my ignorance. I should have figured that there would be a clearing house for actors and stuntmen. They couldn't just appear at the gates and expect to get in. I thanked the guy for giving me a place to go, paid my check, and left. Baggy pants was nowhere in sight.

It looked like the day would turn out to be a scorcher. A hot wind was already blowing down the valley, and it was only a little after ten. There were only a few wispy clouds in a mostly blue sky. I could see why so many people lived there.

I found the place the restaurant guy had told me about. It was an old building out toward one-o-one on the south side of the city. There were a few men milling around outside the door as I walked in. Some empty chairs lined the walls near the entrance, and on the back wall was something similar to a ticket counter. The opening was screened, and a middle-aged man waited behind it.

As I walked up, the guy said loudly, "You're a little late buster. All the jobs are filled for today."

"That's not why I'm here." I said just as loud. I was afraid he might be hard of hearing. "I'm looking for someone."

"Does this look like an information booth?" Now he was becoming belligerent.

I decided to try a different approach. I softened my voice. "I'm sorry. I didn't mean to be loud, but you're my last hope of finding my brother." I used the same story that had worked once before.

He relaxed a little too. "What makes you think he'd be here?"

"I tracked him this far out of Virginia, but then I lost him." I decided to be truthful, at least about that. "His name's Jeb Lee. He might have been a stunt cowboy."

"Yeah, I remember him!" The man in the cage replied, a little excited-as if he had solved a mystery. "But that was a long time ago, back in the thirties, I think. I remember thinking that he had picked a great stage name. But he left town when Magistrate studios folded. At least he said he was getting out of Hollywood, going to Reno. I haven't seen him since."

"Do you know why he would go to Reno?"

"No, it's been too long."

"I can understand that. It's like I've been tailing a ghost. He's not only been one step ahead of me, but almost twenty years. Thanks for your help, though. You've given me more to go on than anyone yet."

It was disappointing that I didn't find Phillip/Jeb, and wrap up my work, so I could collect my fee, and get on with my life. Maybe even go back to Richmond to see Rachel, and find out if there was something between us after all, and not just in my head.

On the other hand, I had one more place to go. I called the car rental agency to see if I could keep the vehicle and return it in Reno. They were accommodating, so I left that afternoon heading north. Why wait. There was nothing for me in Southern California.

Chapter Twenty-Five

The trip to Reno was a pretty one, especially going over the Sierras. I'd never been there before. Mt. Lassen was quite a spectacle, with its snow cap. I sort of wished I'd gone by way of Lake Tahoe, but then I was in a hurry to wrap up my search. When I arrived in town my impatience showed. I changed my approach by driving directly to the rodeo grounds. There would be plenty of time to find a place to stay, hopefully for only one night. It had been a long journey, from Richmond to Nacogdoches, to Hollywood, and now Reno Nevada. Jeb Lee had become an enigma. He filled all my thoughts. He had gotten into my soul. Now I just wanted to end it, and return to some semblance of a life, maybe a life that included Rachel Embree. I missed her, and I really didn't know her. There was just something there, but I didn't know what it was.

The rodeo grounds appeared empty as I drove into the parking lot. There was no sound at all. Of course it was off-season. The snow had barely left the ground. I'd seen traces of it as I passed over the Sierras. The rodeo season was still a month away.

I decided to wander around to see if there were any signs of life. It was a big place. I'd been searching for over five minutes before I heard muffled voices coming from a light linoleum floor, I saw three people behind a counter topped with formica. They stopped talking when they saw me. I was obviously not a local, with my blue slacks, white open-collared shirt and gray hat. My tan, or lack of it, didn't match theirs either.

The only woman in the room rose from her chair at a wooden desk near the back of the room and came up to the counter opposite where I stood. "Can I help you sir?" She had a pleasant voice.

She was a young thing, maybe nineteen or twenty. "I'm looking for somebody," I began, "His name's Jeb Lee. He may be a rodeo performer here. I'm not really sure. I had no idea how the rodeo worked   He'd be around forty now, and average size.

She smiled, "I don't know any of the rodeo riders. It seems like forty would be a little old for a performer. At any rate I'm just here to do some bookwork."

"How about your friends?" I was hopeful. They looked a little older than her.

"No. They're not with the rodeo. They just came to see me." She answered.

I could believe that. She was a cute little thing, but too young for my taste. The two guys seemed interested, but didn't say anything. I was getting the feeling that this was just another dead-end, but I tried one more time, "Have you heard of an Indian named Charlie?" There was no sign of recognition on any of their faces.

"Sorry, no." was all she said as the others shook their head.

I apologized for disturbing them, and walked back out to the parking lot where my rental car was still the only one there. As I drove away I noticed a blue ford parked on the street that I was sure hadn't been there before. It looked empty at first glance, but then I saw someone slouched down in the driver's seat. I thought about stopping to confront him, thinking it was the same man I saw in Hollywood, but then I remembered that I didn't have a license to carry a gun in Nevada, and I might need one if this guy harbored a grudge. Why would he follow me from California for any other reason? I was sure I'd never seen him before that last time. I couldn't figure it out. Maybe I was just being paranoid. The guy could be sleeping one off, and not even know who I was. At any rate, I decided to let him make the first move if I was, in fact, on his enemies list. If he was a pro he wasn't very smart. I spotted him right away.

My next move was a no-brainer, but I didn't think of it right away. What does that say about me? I found a phone booth back in town on Virginia Street and looked up the name Lee.

There were five entries, including a business, Lee Saddlery, which was listed on Virginia Street, only a few blocks from my location, if the numbers were any indication. I decided that would be my first stop, since it was so close.

I left the car parked where it was, and walked to the shop. As my luck would have it, the place was closed. It was open on Saturday and Sunday. So to compensate, it was closed on Tuesday and Wednesday. This was Tuesday.

At that point I decided to check into a hotel. There were plenty on Virginia Street to choose from. There was one called the Golden Horseshoe. If anything would change my luck, it had to be a golden horseshoe, so that's the one I chose. I had to wander through a casino with clanging slot machines to find the hotel registration desk. Luckily there were very few people checking in.

When I got to my room on the fourth floor, I decided to take a shower to clear my head. I had as many as five calls to make.

It was about three in the afternoon when I finally sat on the bed next to the phone, with the phone book open to the L's.

The first listing was for a David Lee. I dialed the number. A woman answered on the third ring. She sounded old as she said "Hello?"

I gave her my spiel about looking for Jeb Lee, and she said she had never heard of him. I thanked her, and apologized for her inconvenience before hanging up. One down.

On the second try there was no answer. Ditto the third. The fourth was obviously oriental. On my fifth call I finally heard a man's voice. He sounded somewhat irritated that I had interrupted him while he was watching a western movie on the television. He called me a few names I had heard before and hung up. I didn't think this was my guy.

It looked like I would have to extend my stay another day so I called the front desk. They said no problem. I'm sure they wanted my slot money. If I was going to gamble it wouldn't be slots. I looked for a little more entertainment for my money, and had been known for shooting craps, an affliction I picked up in the Marine Corps. But I had other things on my mind this trip. There would be no gambling.

I managed to get a good night's sleep, in spite of the drunks in the hall, with their loud mouths. I had breakfast at a casino restaurant, and it was pretty good, and cheap. They made their money off the drunks who gambled, their wallets loosened by the free booze. Since local phone calls were free, I returned to my room after my meal.

One of the phone numbers I had called with no answer was listed as a Margaret Lee. I dialed that one. A boy who sounded like a teen-ager answered.

"Is your dad there?" I asked, holding my breath.

"No."

I pressed on, "How about your mother?"

"No."

This kid had a great vocabulary, I thought.

I decided to try one more thing, "Is your father Jeb Lee?"

There was a silence on the other end for a few seconds, and then a click as the line went dead. I was pretty sure I had the right Lee this time. It was about time. I checked the street address in the phone book, and hurried out to get the rental car, which was in covered parking just next door to the hotel casino. Then it occurred to me that I had no idea where the address was. I was so flustered to finally have a destination that my mind just went blank.

The desk clerk was again very helpful. He gave me precise directions. The house I was looking for was about three miles out of town, northwest on the way to Susanville. In about ten minutes I was parking outside a small wood frame house on a tree-lined dead-end street that only held five more residences. There was no one else around, and only one other car. As I walked up to a small porch I noticed another vehicle just turning onto the same street. I rang the bell and waited.

When the door opened I was looking at a woman about my age. She was wearing an apron. I thought I might have interrupted her cooking something. She gave me a warm smile and asked, "May I help you?"

She was tall for a woman, maybe five-seven, and had a slim build, as far as I could tell. "Are you Mrs. Jeb Lee?" I asked.

Her smile turned to a frown. "I was." She answered, curtly.

I decided to be truthful with this woman, whom I liked immediately, "I've been hired to find your husband. I've come a long way."

I was surprised when she said, "Won't you come in, Mr?" she let it trail off. She seemed very trusting. Maybe it was that kind of neighborhood.

"Dunn, my name is Ivan Dunn." I finished it for her. "And I'd like very much to come in and talk to you."

She opened the screen door, and I walked into a small living room, with a davenport and two chairs. There was a small coffee table strategically placed in front of the couch. I sat in one of the chairs, and Mrs. Lee sat in the other which was facing me.

"What do you want with my husband, Mr. Dunn?"

"I was just hired to find him. I'm not sure why."

Another frown came over her face. "Who hired you?" It was a natural question.

"A Jeremy Taylor in Chicago. I think he's a lawyer, but I'm not sure.

"That's strange," she continued. Just then there was a knock on the door, which she had closed behind us.

"Excuse me for a minute, Mr. Dunn." She said politely, as she rose and went to her front door.

I got up to be polite, and as I did, I glanced out the Lee's living room window toward the street. There parked right behind my car was the other vehicle from the rodeo parking lot. I quickly moved to behind the door that Margaret Lee was pulling open, not knowing what to expect. She glanced at me quizzically, but she opened the door anyway. At that point I was sure she knew there was danger but didn't know which one of us posed the greatest threat.

Chapter Twenty-Six

When Margaret Lee opened her door, the man in baggy pants pushed his way in, gun drawn. She fell backwards onto a scatter rug. When I saw the pistol I quickly slammed my left arm down on the assailant's gun arm. The piece fell to the floor, as the man winced in obvious pain. I immediately wrapped my arms around him so that he couldn't break free, yelling at the woman on the floor to get the firearm. She obeyed, and picking it up by the handle, she aimed it in the direction of the intruder.

. I let the man go and quickly retrieved the revolver from her. The whole episode took only two minutes. "Call the police, quickly." I told Margaret Lee, rather excitedly, and then commanded the intruder to sit on the rug. He complied without saying a word. In fact from the time the whole incident began until the police arrived and took him away, he had said nothing.

When we were once again alone in the room, I looked at her with approval, saying, "You were pretty good back there Mrs. Lee."

"Please call me Margaret. I can't stop shaking."

"You should sit down. Nobody is prepared for that sort of experience." I said, trying to calm her.

"No. I suppose not. Do you know who he is?" She asked

"I do not. I'll check with the police later and try to find out for you. All I know is that I first noticed him in Hollywood. He must have followed me here. Maybe it has something to do with your husband. He could have confronted me before this." I was just as puzzled as she was.

"I don't understand any of this." She said.

I answered, "I wish I could shed light on it for you. I don't know what's going on either. I guess we'll both just have to wait for the police report."

For the first time I really looked around the room. On a mantle over a fireplace was a picture frame that held some sort of medal. I curiously walked over to it, and recognized it right away. It was the same medal I was awarded when my knee was shattered.

"That's my husband's Purple Heart." She said with a proud tone to her voice.

I was surprised. "I didn't know he was in the service."

"He earned it at the Battle of the Coral Sea. He was in the Navy."

"Please tell me about it. You must be very proud." I said, leaning intently forward on my seat.

"I was. I loved my husband very much." And then she told the incredible story of what happened to Jeb Lee.

It was 1933, in the heart of the depression when Margaret met the flamboyant cowboy Jeb Lee. She, like everyone else, was worried about her future. He strode into her father's bank that day as if he owned the world. He wasn't dressed like the other customers. He wore boots and jeans, with a plaid shirt, topped off with a ten-gallon white hat. It was as if he had just stepped out of a movie. He was Tom Mix, at least to the impressionable girl.

After the introduction by her father, the romance blossomed quickly. He was not much taller than her, but he was muscular, probably gleaned from his days as a ranch-hand in Texas. She had never met anyone quite like the soft-spoken man with the Texas drawl. She didn't know about his past, and didn't really care. Later, after they were married, he would tell her about the ranch life, but not about Virginia, and the train ride west.

He also left out the part about Celia Devin.

The courtship could be considered whirlwind. They were married in June of that year. A son, Mathew, followed eight months later.

Jeb split his time between his rodeo chores, which were limited to a rope trick segment, and duties as a clown, rescuing riders from a possible death from goring when they were thrown, and Lee Saddlery, the business her father had bought for his new son-in-law.

Charlie Redbird stopped by once in a while, too often for Margaret's taste, to reminisce about the rodeo, of which they both were a part, and to drink beer. Margaret hated the smell of beer, and often denied her husband in bed when he had been drinking. Of course that infuriated him in his condition. It was then that he felt more amorous.

It wasn't long before Jeb began seeking affection elsewhere. He would come home from work at the shop on Virginia Street much later than normal, nearly always with the stench of alcohol on his breath.

Margaret was not unaware of his dalliances, but she put up with it for the sake of their son. And she still loved him, in spite of everything.

They were just drifting along late in 1941 when Japan attacked Pearl Harbor. Maybe it was patriotism that made Jeb enlist in the

Navy. Or perhaps it was his deteriorating home life. He could have gotten a deferment because he had a family. Instead he chose to join. Charlie Redbird followed suit.

They took the train to boot camp in San Diego together. Both men were in good shape from their chosen profession, so they sailed through the training effortlessly. Upon graduation they were assigned to the destroyer Sims together.

Things were moving fast in 1942. The Japanese had conquered the Phillipines, and were making advances in the rest of the western hemisphere. Many in the United States felt that they couldn't be stopped. There was fear that the west coast would be attacked. Then in May came the battle of the Coral Sea.

"You have to realize that much of this I got from one of Jeb's shipmates who survived and came to see me after the war. Of the one hundred and ninety-two officers and men aboard the Sims, only fourteen survived." Margaret related.

I remembered that Annie's fiancé had been assigned to the Sims. The odds were not good that he would be one of the fourteen who lived. I would have liked to call her and offer my sympathy, but I had no idea where she would be. I wondered if the officer had known Jeb.

They certainly wouldn't have been friends, with the class distinction between officers and enlisted. It seemed ironic to me that they would be companions in death, but not in life.

Just then the phone rang, bringing me back to the present. "It was the police", Margaret said, after hanging up. "They wrung a full confession from our assailant. It seems he was engaged to marry one Celia Devin, when Jeb Lee stole her from him. He vowed to get even. When you showed up looking for the same guy, he followed you. It wasn't Romeo and Juliet, but he was serious, and a little deranged. They just thought we'd like to know." I remember thinking there are sure a lot of whackos in this world. How could you hold a grudge for that long?

"So it's 1942, and Jeb with his sidekick Charlie Redbird are on the destroyer USS Sims heading into the Coral Sea. Then what?" I was on the edge of my chair. I'd come a long way to hear this story.

"Do you know anything about that battle?" She continued.

I thought about it, "The only thing I remember is that we won." I was a little busy at the time with the Marines.

"Really it was a kind of a draw. We did win in the long run though. It weakened the

Japanese forces enough that we had the advantage at Midway." She related.

She knew a lot more about it than I did. "So what happened?"

"Jeb was a boatswain's mate striker, so he was mostly up on deck. Charlie on the other hand became an engineman, and you know where the engines are." She continued.

"All I know is that I don't know anything about ships, except that they carried the Marines to the most god-awful places in the world." I answered, flippantly.

"Well, Charlie was way below decks", she said, "and a Jap dive bomber scored a direct hit on their ship. It actually broke apart before sinking. From what Jeb's friend told me, my husband tried to get to Charlie instead of abandoning ship when he had the chance." She paused, and took a deep breath, "They both went down with the ship. Their bodies were never recovered." Tears came to Margaret's eyes, and then her body was wracked with sobs.

I went to her and put my arms around her. There wasn't much I could say, except, "I'm so sorry!" And I meant it. At that time in Phillip Atchison's life, he wasn't a bum in my mind but a genuine hero. The sins of his past were washed away as he went to his maker.

I thanked Margaret Lee for her help in ending my journey to find the truth, and told her I was glad that I met her. She was quite a lady.

I caught a flight out that night for San Francisco, where I had to make the connection to go on to Chicago.

Chapter Twenty-Seven

So here I was, heading back to where it had all begun. I had a bitter taste in my mouth for the way it ended. Phillip Atchison the third had started out an idealistic kid in love, and then turned into a killer through no fault of his own. Circumstance devoured the young man. But then Jeb Lee became a hero in his final moments. He was a credit to the namesakes he had chosen; Jeb Stuart and General Robert E. Lee, the pride of the South of long ago.

I had called my employer, whoever he or she was, to say that I had the entire story. I was told to return to Chicago and was given the address at which to make my report, and pick up my money. I was anxious for it to be over, so I flew back to the windy city from Reno.

I took a cab to where my beat-up Chevy was stored, and then headed north. It was a warm sunny day for a change, and I rolled down both my front windows to let the breeze cool me.

Once I was inside the huge mansion in the woods, a servant led me to a large study, telling me the master of the house would join me shortly. The whole setup smelled of money.

After only a few moments the same man who had met me came through one of the two openings pushing an older woman in a wheelchair into the room until she was only a few feet from me. When she spoke she had a husky strong voice that belied her age, which I guessed to be about sixty-five.

"I am happy to meet you Mister Dunopolous. It's been quite a while since I hired you." She smiled broadly,

I was shocked that she knew my real name. I hadn't told Jeremy Taylor. "You have me at a disadvantage. I have no idea who you are." I answered. I hoped it didn't sound rude.

"My name is Elizabeth Brecker, but I'm sure that won't mean anything to you."

She was right about that. "I'm sorry. No it doesn't."

She continued, "That's all right. Everything will be made clear to you shortly. Tell me about Phillip."

"It's hard to know where to start." Then I just blurted it out. "He's dead." I looked in her eyes, but there was no reaction, so I continued, "He died a hero, trying to save a buddy on the ship he went to war in." Then I went back to the beginning, at the bank in Richmond. I laid out the whole thing for her as her eyes turned sad, and her body slumped slowly. When I finished she sighed, and handed me an envelope. She then turned the motor-less vehicle of her incarceration and wheeled herself back out of the room.

I didn't know whether I was supposed to just leave, or sit there and examine the contents of the envelope, which I presumed was my final payment. I decided to go, but before I could get out of the study, the man-servant who had brought me there came back. He courteously led me to the entrance, said goodbye and closed the door behind me.

I went back to my car, bewildered. It was as if the whole project had been worthless. What was the point? I drove back into the city and went to my office, on which I had kept up the lease payments the whole time I was gone.

Suddenly I felt hungry. I hadn't eaten anything all day. I'd been so anxious to share all that I had learned with someone that I had forgotten about food. I called the corner Delicatessen and ordered a pastrami and swiss on rye. Then I just sat there waiting, and looking at the envelope I had been handed by Miss or Mrs. Brecker. I didn't know anything about her. I still didn't know her interest in all this.

When the boy came with my sandwich I wolfed it down, wishing I had ordered two.

Then I turned my attention back to the envelope on the desk in front of me.

The first thing I noticed when I opened it was some folded paper. It seemed to be a letter. Inside the paper was a check for Thirty-five thousand dollars. I thought that was extremely generous, since I hadn't earned nearly that much with my expenses. It was in addition to the retainer Jeremy Taylor had given me. Perhaps the letter would explain the extra bonus, and what it all meant to Elizabeth Brecker, if that really was her name.

Dear Ivan,

I know you have many questions about why you were hired, and who, in fact, hired you. Perhaps this will explain everything. I am Phillip's Mother. I always wondered what happened to him, though I was pretty sure he was dead. Thank you for easing the pain of an old woman. Believe me the answers you provided are worth much more to me than you were paid. I was proud of my son when he was a child, and I'm even more impressed with his accomplishments now. I only wish I could have buried him with his dear father.

Now on to some unfinished business. I couldn't tell you to your face. I suppose I am a coward. I knew your full name because I was in love with your father, Eric Dunopolous! It was very awkward because I was married to Phillip Atchison the second at the time. I cared for Phillip too, but not the way I loved Eric. We met by chance, and the affair was brief. He broke it off because he was an honorable man. He didn't know I was married when we became lovers. A baby was born of this union. I had left Phillip when I realized I was with child. It was a boy. We named him Ivan! Eric took the baby, by mutual consent. Phillip took me back, and soon we had our own child, who we named Phillip. So you see, you are my son, and you were Phillip the third's brother.

I am dying, son. I've known it for quite a while now. You are the sole heir to my fortune, which is considerable. I have been very fortunate in financial matters over the years. I am including the name and address of my attorneys. They have been advised to contact you when I am gone.

Don't ever doubt that I have always loved you. I have watched you from afar, and even seen you from time to time. I am very proud of you, and have no regrets.

Love, Elizabeth Atchison-Brecker

I was numb. I couldn't breathe. How could I go through forty years of life not knowing? Then sadness took over. Why had I not been told before. I could understand it when I was a child, but later it would have made so much difference. I'd been told my mother had died. I remember how badly I had felt. I was only four, and I cried. The memory of that day made the betrayal I lived through all the rest of my childhood, and my adult life until now, hurt so much. Perhaps Elizabeth Brecker knew that she couldn't bridge so large a gap in my life, and that's why she chose to write a letter. Maybe she understood that it was too late for us. I'm not sure that a relationship would be possible at this stage in our lives. I felt sorry that she was ill, and might not survive, but to go back to her home now was not an option I thought I had. Her goodbye had sounded like a dismissal. I was willing to leave it at that, at least for now.

I had a brother! That would have changed so many things. Then another reality struck me. I was Thomas Embree's Uncle! How would Rachel feel about that?

Suddenly I wanted to be there, in Richmond, to tell her. I wanted to hold her close and ask her to marry me. Certainly money was no longer a problem.

I called the airline and made reservations for Richmond in a week. It would take me that long to close up shop here, and pay my bills. Then something occurred to me, and I smiled to myself. If I pulled this off, I would upgrade from Uncle to being Thomas Embree's Step-Father. I would have my family after all.

The end of a Novel by
Frank A. Perdue

Lost in the Shadows

an Ivan Dunn Mystery

Chapter One

It began as a whim; a momentary lapse in judgment. I could have just driven by, and my life would have been so much easier. That's what I would have done if his sign was the same as all the others. You see these guys at just about every intersection these days, but back in 1952 it was a novelty. The movement, if you could call it that, hadn't really gotten started yet. The American dream of a house, a car, two kids and a dog or cat was still a reality to most, and everyone was hard at work to achieve it.

The sign on a busy street corner was just a dream of one person; a way to extract our hard-earned dollars. Or it could be that the first one really needed the dough. He could have been a war hero, out of luck, with no family to turn to. Not knowing where his next meal was coming from. Or if there would be a next meal.

Even if I had seen that first guy I would have driven by. I didn't have any money in those days. I don't know if it started in Chicago or not, but that's where I was when I saw the first one. His crudely drawn sign, probably on a piece of cardboard that he had rummaged out of someone's trash, could have said something like, "Out of Work, and Starving. Please Help." I don't remember because I drove by trying not to make eye contact.

Before Jeremy Taylor sauntered into my cheap office, I only had enough money for a few weeks. I didn't even have a secretary. I was dressed a little better though. I was trying to make an impression. It turned out that the case he offered me brought me fortune if not fame. Some of the money I had earned, but not all. Anyway that's another story.

Before I got lucky I could have been that guy on the street corner. So maybe that's why I talked to this fellow, but I prefer to think it was his sign, drawn on a piece of cardboard with a black marker. It read, "Buy me lunch and I'll tell you my story."

This guy was dressed pretty much the same as the others; dusty-looking dungarees, and a plaid shirt with what looked like moth holes up near the collar. His hair was long, not even braided. He wore sandals that didn't go with the rest of him. Granted, we were in the beach town of San Diego, but it was January, with the temperature that morning hovering around forty. He wore no jacket. It made no sense, my stopping that is.

My whole perspective had changed in just two short years. So had the world for that matter. Early in 1950 the communist North Koreans were still above the 38th parallel. I lived in the windy city of Chicago, and Rachel Embree didn't exist as far as I was concerned. Contrast that to now; The war was raging, no longer called a "Police Action", and I was in the beautiful city along the Southern

185

California coast living that dream, except for the kids and pet, and a little thing called a marriage certificate. I was working on that.

I was a little too old to fight. Besides I'd had my war. Now that I had money, lots of it, I was semi-retired. My private detective career, short as it was, was a thing of the past.

The panhandler jumped eagerly into my old Studebaker as car horns behind me shrieked in unison. In the old days I would have raised my middle finger suggestively, but I was much smarter now.

I'd picked up my passenger on Harbor Drive near the civic center, so I made a u-turn and headed out toward the ocean. There was a little café in Ocean Beach that I liked. They didn't serve liquor or beer, which I thought was a good idea under the circumstances.

We found a fairly quiet table near the back, and ordered non-alcoholic drinks when the pretty waitress came by. Right away my companion excused himself to go to the restroom. I studied the man as he walked away. He had no obvious physical impairments. The first time he talked was when we ordered at the café. He had a clear deep voice that showed no sign of despair. It didn't compute. He was reasonably tall, around six feet. There didn't seem to be an ounce of fat on his muscular frame.

When he returned and we had ordered, I said, "Okay, we have a few minutes, so talk to me. What's going on with you?"

He looked me square in the eyes and answered, unhesitatingly, "I wish I knew. Up until a week ago, I didn't exist, as far as I know. I woke up soaking wet, in Chicago by the lake, with a ringing headache. I have no idea how I got there, or what happened before that."

"Do you know your name?" I interrupted.

"No." He said, simply.

"How did you get to San Diego?" I said, and then as an afterthought, "And why?"

"There was a piece of paper in my pocket. It was all I had on me. I could hardly read it, because of the dampness, but it was an address here in the city. It was my only lead to who I am." He paused to catch his breath. "I hitchhiked out here."

We stopped to eat when the waitress brought our food. My companion wolfed his down before I had finished my salad. I asked if he wanted something else. He finished off two plates but he politely declined a third. It just didn't fit. He seemed a little too courteous for a street guy. I couldn't tell whether he was lying about his loss of memory or not.

"Go on", I said. "I can finish eating and listen at the same time. What did you find at the address you had?"

"It was the Longshoreman's union hall. No one there knew me. As long as I was there I asked them for a job on the docks but they had nothing for me." He answered dejectedly, dropping his head. "I had nowhere else to go."

I had a thought. "Where did you get the fine duds?"

He ignored the sarcasm and answered, "One of the guys at the hall gave them to me. I thought then that they might hire me out of pity, which would have been alright with me but, as I said, that didn't work out either. That was my only lead, and I didn't know where to go from there."

"So did you go right out and make your sign?" It was an honest question on my part, but it must have sounded trite, because he got a disgusted look on his face before he answered.

"No. I was able to get temporary work at a department store, cleaning up after the holiday rush. I only worked nights. I suppose it was so that no one would see me. The job only lasted three days."

"So why the sign?"

"Simple really. I haven't eaten in a couple of days, and I had no one to turn to." It seemed like an honest statement. "I figured I'd worry about the rest of my life on a full stomach, if that was possible."

I thought of something, "I have to call you something. Hey you won't do. How about Joe? What do you think of that name?

"I suppose it's as good as any," he replied.

I made a decision then that, in light of what happened later, had to be the worst ever. "I have some experience in detective work, and I'm at leisure these days, so here's what I'd like to do. I'll put you up at my place temporarily.

I have an empty guest house. Meanwhile let me do some poking around and see what I can find out about who you are. Will that be all right with you?"

He was incredulous. "How could I say no to that? You might have just saved my life." I remember thinking at the time that maybe he was being overdramatic. As things turned out it was just the opposite!

Chapter Two

It was a short ride through Pacific Beach to the La Jolla hills where I now resided, in the lap of luxury. Joe was impressed, especially looking back along the beach as we climbed. It was a pretty sight, with the Point Loma peninsula stretching out toward Mexico. I'd been saying to myself a lot these last few weeks, "Ivan Dunn you are a lucky son of a gun!"

My Studebaker didn't really match up with my surroundings, and I'd gotten a few disapproving looks from the neighbors, but I was used to it, and didn't yet feel really rich, though I was. Maybe I'd get a second car one of these days, but I wouldn't sell the one I had. It was comfortable. Rachel kidded that I liked it because I didn't know whether I was coming or going. If you've never seen an old Studebaker, the front end looks just like the back, with the cab in between.

When I pulled onto the winding driveway leading to the big house, I wondered if Rachel would approve of our new house guest. She was pretty broad-minded, so I hoped it would be okay.

Rachel Embree had moved out to the coast right after her son Thomas returned to the Army. He'd gotten a hardship discharge when he was needed at home, but had it rescinded when the crisis was resolved. After he left she had nothing but bad memories to keep her in Richmond, so she packed up and moved to the west coast, at my selfish suggestion. It would be a new start. I had saved her life, and I was sure she had feelings for me. It wasn't hard at all to ask her to move in with me. She would have her own room, and I assured her I would stay at arm's length. She worried about what the neighbors might think, but when she saw how secluded my place was, she decided it would be all right- until she could find her own apartment.

That was a year ago, and lucky for me, she was still here. She wanted to find a job, but I kept talking her out of it. I told her it was unnecessary, since I had all the money in the world. She could always do it later, if she became bored with the life, or with me.

I was becoming accustomed to the domesticated life again. Had it really been ten years since I put Annie on that bus to Boston?

Annie and I had been very young when we were married. We both became different people as the years ticked by. I changed more than her, and not for the better. We split up just before the Japs bombed Pearl Harbor.

When the man I called Joe and I reached the front door of the huge house, it opened and Rachel stood there, an inquisitive look on her pretty face. I continually marveled at her beauty. Her dark, nearly black hair, that she had cut short since she moved to the warmer climate of Southern California, framed her beauty well. Her slim body on a five-foot ten frame was just right for me, since I was nudging six feet .

"This is Joe," I said, anticipating her question. "He's going to rent the guest house for a while." It was just a small lie, and I would straighten it out with her later, in private.

Rachel held out her hand to him, and he shook it, very formally, and, I might add, slightly ill at ease.

As I observed the two of them I noticed that Joe was very pale, almost waxen, but that could be due to his diet, or lack of one. Otherwise he was a good looking guy with long brown hair combed straight back with no part. His jaw was rather pointed. His nose appeared to have been broken, but was not unsightly. One thing that seemed out of place, other than his clothes, was his eyes. They were a steely blue. When he looked at me I had the feeling he was looking right through me.

I was yanked back to the moment when I realized Rachel was speaking. "Have you eaten, Joe? I can make some sandwiches if you're interested."

"No thanks Rachel. May I call you that?" He was awfully courteous for a homeless guy. There had to be more to him than I knew.

She smiled and answered in the affirmative. "How about you Ivan? Are you hungry?"

"We just ate, but thanks," I replied. "I'm going to take Joe out to the guest house and get him settled."

There was a back door to the big house that was separated from the smaller structure by a porch and short walkway. There was no side door to the guest house. It had only one floor, as opposed to the main building which had three. A three-car garage sat on the other side of the big house from the guest cottage. Rachel had her own car, a '51 Ford, which I had bought for her when she arrived on my doorstep. It was parked in the garage.

After showing Joe around his new digs, I headed back to the main house to answer Rachel's obvious questions.

"Okay, what's going on?" She asked, as soon as I entered. I explained the whole thing in as much detail as I could muster.

"How are you going to help him?" She continued.

I thought for a second before answering, "I'm not sure, but I don't think I'll find the answer here. What would you think if I went to Chicago?"

"I'd say you are being foolish right offhand, but you have to do what you think is best." Then she added, turning away from me, "It's not like you have anything to hold you here."

I reacted by grabbing her by the shoulders, making her look at me, "You know that's not true. You've become my life!"

She turned her face upward, and placed her left hand behind my neck, "Oh Ivan, I know it's been hard for you these past months, and I appreciate what you've done for me. I feel I'm at least moving back into the world from where I've been."

I grinned, "How far back?"

"This far", she answered, pulling my head so that her lips were close to mine. She closed her eyes as I completed the union between us. Her mouth opened slightly, suggesting that she wanted more from me.

I had to be careful to let her lead with what she was willing to give, lest she be frightened back to that other world, the one that she had been trapped in ever since she'd been assaulted. Up until now I'd made no demands on her, sexually or otherwise. I was trying to be content just being near her. But now my male hormones were getting in the way, and I pressed against her, harder than I probably should have.

Suddenly she pulled away, but her eyes never left me. She appeared to be fighting with herself over which way to go. I realized I had won when she took the step that brought her back to me. Our second kiss was much more passionate than the first, as she molded her frame to mine, and we both became lost in the embrace.

Rachel said nothing as I lifted her while she wrapped her slim legs around me. I carried her up a flight of stairs to my room, where we fell on the bed still entwined.

I kissed the spot just behind her collarbone near the base of her neck, and she moaned appreciatively. Her hands went to my belt, and I stopped her. It was the hardest thing I've ever done. I could feel her trembling as she looked up at me questioningly.

"I'm in love with you Rachel. I have been for over a year. I'm not a monk, but I want this to be perfect." Then I voiced the thought that had been on my mind ever since I found out I would have money. "Will you marry me?"

She took a deep breath before answering. "I'm a hussy Ivan. I've never wanted anything so much in my life. I don't deserve you, but the answer is yes. Will tomorrow be soon enough?"

Chapter Three

In California there is a three day waiting period that begins after applying for a marriage license. I was going to use that time to fly to Chicago and see what I could dig up on our John Doe, conveniently named Joe, which, I never thought of before, was a combination of the other two names. Brilliant. While I was gone my beautiful Rachel was going shopping for wedding dresses.

The Pan Am flight I caught left from Los Angeles, and only made three stops before reaching Chicago. I had taken a commuter flight north to L.A after Rachel dropped me off at Lindbergh Field, I would use a cab in the windy city for what I thought would be only a one or two day investigation.

I checked into a downtown hotel. After showering, I called the AAA cab company to pick me up. They were the same ones who drove me from the airport, and who were helpful in finding a good hotel. I also received a crash course in Illinois politics from my driver. I felt I owed them my business in spite of it.

I wanted to check with the police to see if they had any record of a missing person fitting the description of Joe. After that I'd visit the local library to scan old copies of the newspaper for information that might fit.

Come right down to it, I didn't have much of a plan for later. Maybe I would go by the Longshoremen's Union in town, if there was one. In my mind I was a hotshot investigator, so it was time to prove it. At least I knew where most everything was, having lived here before. The downtown area hadn't changed much, save for a few name changes on things like hotels.

I couldn't have picked a worse time to bother the cops with my problem. One of their own had been shot and killed the night before, and the gunman was still on the loose. They had no time for me and let me know it right away. They used some choice words to explain what they thought of PI's. I didn't mind.

I had tried to join the force when I mustered out of the Marines, but the injury I suffered to my knee from the action on Makin Island in 1942 kept me from passing the physical. The esprit de corps we had was pretty much the same in the police. When we lost one of our own we all suffered, and we tried never to leave a fallen buddy on the battlefield.

Recovering from my wound at the Naval Hospital in San Diego allowed me time to fall in love with the area. I had always wanted to return, and when I inherited a fortune from the estate of my mother I made the move. Now here I was back where I had started, and I was lost.

The Chicago Daily News turned out to be a dead end. In the week following when Joe had said he emerged from Lake Michigan, there was not one story about a near drowning. No one had been reported missing, as far as the newspaper was concerned. So I was zero for two.

I had no luck at the Longshoremen's hall either. There was only one guy there. I told him my name and I showed him the same picture I had flashed at the police station, the one I had hurriedly snapped before I left for Chicago. At least he looked at it.

"That's not one of our guys", he had said, with a blank look on his face. He didn't offer any more than that, before he returned to his comic book.

I had one more idea before I packed it in and flew back to paradise on the west coast, but it would have to wait until the next day. I was bushed. I think it was because I seemed to be at a dead end. At any rate, sleep sounded like a good idea.

Before heading back to my hotel I decided I had better rent a car after all. I didn't feel like throwing more money away on a cab, since by that time I realized I would have to drive out to the lake where Joe had his near death experience. And it would be more convenient.

I awoke late because the brightness of the new day was blocked by heavy drapes in my room. After showering I sauntered down to the coffee shop just off the hotel lobby, and ordered my usual of ham and eggs with Tabasco hot sauce. I liked my food spicy. I often thought I must have some Mexican or

Spanish blood, but my name implied I was Greek.

After arranging for the rental car I drove down to the lake and headed north along the shore. Joe said he woke up about thirty miles north of the city in a park along the waterfront. I wanted to try to find the spot, and see if anything jumped out at me. Maybe someone there had seen something, even though they hadn't reported it.

I'd been driving for about forty-five minutes when I spotted the sign. It was simple and to the point. It read 'North City Park' with an arrow pointing in the direction of Lake Michigan. I made the turn, and in just a few city blocks I reached a grassy area with a couple of empty benches, and a sidewalk paralleling the water's edge. The whole park couldn't have been more than one hundred feet wide and not much deeper than that. There were large houses on either side that I would classify as mansions. The one north of the park had huge round white pillars reaching from the porch to the eaves of the huge encompassing roof. I wondered how the city had managed to secure such a prime location for its park.

I left the car and took a pathway down to the beach where a lone fisherman sat on a stone wall separating the park from the lake.

He must have heard me because he turned and looked my way as I approached. "Hello there", was his greeting. He appeared to be in his seventies, with white hair protruding from his floppy wide-brimmed hat that I imagined was to keep the Sun from his rather large nose.

"Hi old-timer", I answered. "Do you come here often?"

His eyes, which appeared tired even though it was only about noon, looked me over before answering. "You don't look like no fisherman to me. What brings you down here?"

I hate it when people answer a question with one of their own. Of course he was referring to the fact that I was hatless, and wearing a sport shirt and slacks. My brown polished shoes didn't fit the attire of a fisherman either. I looked more like I just stepped off the Queen Mary cruise ship.

I didn't want the old man to clam up, which was exactly what he might do if he knew I was a detective, so I stretched the truth a little. "A friend of mine was out here a few weeks ago, and he was mugged. He ended up in the hospital, and asked me to see if I could find his wallet. They even took his clothes." I looked him in the eyes to see if he bought my story.

"What day was that?" He was paying more attention now, like he was going to solve the mystery.

"It was the week after Christmas, on a Friday. He had just been paid." I was really getting into this.

His left hand went to his brow, as if he was trying to recall something, "I think I was here that day, but I'm not sure. When you get as old as me, young fella, you forget things. I never saw anything unusual about that time."

I started to respond, but then he stopped me. "There was one thing that puzzled me though, about then." He paused for effect, or maybe to catch his breath. "I came out early one day, about five. I had one of my coughing spells, and was up most of the night, so I decided to get some fishing in, because I couldn't get back to sleep, you see."

I was anxiously waiting for him to get to the point, but I knew I couldn't rush him. "Sure", I said, "Then what happened?"

"I'm getting to that. I have to remember as I go along." He smiled, enjoying the fact that he had me on the hook, like the big fish he had never caught. "I had just cast my line, when I heard it."

"Heard what?" I was becoming impatient.

"Are you in a hurry?" He asked. "I was going to tell you. It sounded like the whole city was on fire, with sirens going off. They kept getting closer, and soon I saw why."

Okay, I was losing it now. "Saw what?" I was exasperated, and threw caution to the wind.

My voice must have raised a few octaves because he threw up his hands and said, "You want me to tell the story or not? I'm getting to it if you'll quit interrupting."

At this point I felt I had better appease this old guy, and quickly. "I'm sorry. Go ahead."

That seemed to settle him back down, or he was just having fun with me, and he was going to finish the story, no matter what. "Okay, where was I? Oh I remember. Before long a fire engine showed up, followed by an ambulance, and a couple of police cars. They all looked around, even out over the water, and then they huddled up like at a football game. I couldn't hear what they was saying, but soon they just climbed back in their vehicles and off they went."

"That does seem strange." Then I had a thought, "Did the cars actually say police, or could it have been the sheriff, or state patrol?"

"Now that you mention it, I'm not sure." He answered. "Could have been one of the others."

I doubted he could give me any more information, so I thanked him and wished him well with his fishing, then I went back to my car. It occurred to me that if there was such a large commotion that day, maybe someone else saw something out of place. I decided to check at the houses on either side of the park. Could be I would get lucky.

I had no such luck. I encountered butlers or man-servants at both locations. They informed me that their masters were out, and they were sure nothing out of the ordinary had been observed. It was as if they saw me coming and coordinated their responses.

When I left the place just north of the park I went to the side of the house and looked up. There was a huge bay window on what appeared to be the third floor. It would have been an ideal location for the curious to see everything that went on along the shore. I couldn't be sure, but it appeared that someone was watching me behind the plate glass. I might have to follow up on that later.

As I was driving back into town I thought about Rachel, and wondered how she was doing with finding a wedding dress. We had decided not to have a large ceremony for a couple of reasons. We didn't know many people in San Diego, and the preparations involved would have taken too much time. We were both anxious to start our married lives right away. It was quite a concession for her. I know how important a big affair is to a woman, of any age. I made a mental note to call her when I got back to the hotel. I would see her the next evening, but still I felt like talking to my beautiful bride to be. I realized that I hadn't called her when I arrived in Chicago. She would probably be upset, and with good reason. It was very thoughtless of me.

There was no answer at the house when I called. I figured she was out shopping, and I would try again later.

I looked up the address of the local library, I knew I wouldn't find anything in the newspapers there, but It would be a good place to pick up addresses I would need, and it wouldn't hurt to question the person behind the desk. One never knows if maybe they might run into a snoop who knows everything. It was still reasonably early in the afternoon, so I might be able to take care of both chores before dark.

The law enforcement office was the closest to my hotel, so I went there first. The deputy was very helpful. He said there was a call about a possible drowning out at the lake by the park, but when they arrived they found nothing.

"Who made the call?" I asked.

"As I remember it was anonymous," was his answer.

I thought about the big window at the house next to the park. I would have been surprised if the call didn't come from there.

I held my breath waiting for the answer to my next question, "Did you find out if anyone was missing? Did anybody call about a disappearance?"

The deputy appeared to be thinking, "No. We checked with the Chicago police, and surrounding towns. Everyone seemed to be accounted for."

I was getting good at reaching dead ends. Every idea I had failed to pan out. I was due for some good luck for a change.

The city library was across town. Time was against me as all the people who worked in town were just leaving for home. Traffic would be a mess. I decided to save the library for the next day. I hadn't booked my flight back to the coast yet so I would call and make reservations for the next evening, when I got back to the hotel That would also give me time to drive back out to the park by the lake, and do some more snooping around.

Chapter Four

The next morning I tried Rachel's number again, keeping in mind the two hour time difference between Chicago and the west coast. I waited until ten-thirty Central time to dial. I was so anxious to talk to her, to hear her melodic voice, that I took a chance on waking her. She must have heard the ring. The phone cradle was right next to her bed, with another in the kitchen. Perhaps she was taking a bath with the door closed. I began to wish I had given her my hotel name and number.

"Relax Ivan," I told myself. "Just call her later." I had already showered and dressed, so I went down to the coffee shop and had breakfast. Then I went back to my room and called her again. She answered on the first ring.

"Darling, I just missed your call earlier, so this time I didn't want to take a chance."

I was relieved. "Did you get your dress okay?

"No. I looked at a few, but I don't want to be hasty. I'd kind of like you to see it before I commit."

"Sure. We'll take care of it as soon as I return." We talked in generalities for a while before hanging up with 'I love you' on both sides.

I drove back out to the park by the lake, and stopped the car about a hundred yards up the street from the large house with the bay window. I was trying to formulate an excuse that would gain me access to the place when a black limousine emerged from a side garage and slowly pulled out onto the street, heading in the direction of the city.

After a few seconds I made a u-turn and began following the large vehicle. I stayed a block behind as the car moved onto the parkway paralleling the lake.

When both cars reached the city it became a little harder to keep them in view. I was assuming there was a chauffeur behind the wheel and the owner of the mansion in the back. I hadn't seen anyone in the passenger seat up front. I crept closer so as to not lose sight of the limo.

Soon the big car pulled up in front of an office. I recognized it right away. I had been there my first day in the Windy City. It was the Longshoremen's Union Hall.

I watched as the uniformed driver went to the rear door facing the building and opened it for his passenger. A man who appeared to be slightly taller than the average emerged wearing an overcoat and fedora tilted low over his face. He seemed to be about my size. I couldn't tell more than that as he went inside the building.

I sat and waited for about a half hour. My quarry didn't come out. Soon the limo without its passenger drove off. I didn't know what to do then, So I waited a little longer. I didn't think the chauffeur could help me.

Finally, running out of options, I went into the Hall. This time there were two people there, neither of them the passenger I was following. I went up to the window where the man I assumed to be a dispatcher was.

"Not you again," he exclaimed in a disgusted tone. "I told you I didn't have any information for you. Now why don't you just get out of here and let me finish my work?"

I'd had enough of this. I reached behind the counter and, grabbing the man by his shirt collar, pulled him to me. "Look bud, I haven't figured out what's going on here yet, but I bet you're right in the middle of it. A man came in here a few minutes ago, but I don't see him now."

The trapped man tried to pull away to no avail. I was quite a bit larger than him. He was giving up maybe forty pounds. "I don't know what you're talking about mister. I never saw anybody. I don't know nothing!"

I was about to describe the man who had entered earlier and mysteriously disappeared, when a voice behind me said, "Sarge. Is that you?"

I released my grip on the little man, and turned to face the voice I had heard. It took a second to recognize the guy, but then it hit me, "Jerry, Jerry Greenway, of all people. What are you doing here? I didn't know you lived in Chicago."

Jerry was a kid out of my past, to whom I owed my life. When the Marines were making their way back to the Nautilus sub after attacking the Japanese on Makin Island in 1942, I was bleeding from a wound to my knee and was in pretty bad shape. When our raft overturned in heavy surf, I would have drowned if private Greenway hadn't held my head above water, and helped me back onto the inflated rubber raft. I might not have made it without his help.

When the sub reached Pearl, I was transported to the hospital, and the Greenway kid was reassigned. We never saw each other again, until now.

He was speaking, "Manny, this is sergeant Ivan Dunnopolous. Manny's not a bad guy Sarge. He's just doing his job."

"It's just Ivan Dunn now kid." Makin was ten years ago, but Greenway still looked like a nineteen year-old. "Do you know anything about this setup?"

"No. I come down every day, and only get about three days work a week, but It lets me keep my financial head above water." He thought for a second and then said, "Do you have time for a beer? Maybe we can catch up."

"Sure. Is there a bar near here?" I was anxious to see if he really knew anything. It could be that he didn't want to say anything in front of that Manny guy.

It turned out there was a place that only served beer and wine about a block away. It
208

wasn't really dark like so many of the saloons I'd been in lately.

We found a table in a corner. There was no one near us. I got to it right away. "Is there another way out of that place? I know a guy went in there, but he didn't come out the front. I was watching."

"There might be. There's a door off to the side I've seen a couple guys go in. While the door was open I could see a large table, like for a conference. There could be another door out of that room to the street. I'm not really sure." Then he thought for a second before continuing, "What did the one you want look like?

He had me there. "I'm not sure. He was wearing an overcoat, pulled up at the collar, and a hat, like a fedora. I never got a look at his face."

Jerry got an excited look on his face. "Yeah, I saw that guy. All I know is he was white. He went through that door I was telling you about. He never spoke to Manny."

Well that solved one mystery. The overcoated one wasn't invisible after all. Now all I had to figure out was what he had to do with anything. I was sure at this point that he fit into the puzzle somewhere. I just didn't know where.

Greenway and I made small talk for a while, catching up on the years between the ocean off Makin Island and now. I told him about Rachel, and the fact I was headed back to San Diego to be married the next day. He said he was still single, but hopeful that the girl he was seeing was the one.

"Her name is Judy Evanson. I'd sure like for you to meet her."

"Yeah, I'd like that."

It was strange that he had been in Chicago all the time I was there, but we never knew it. He was a good kid.

When we said goodbye it was with the promise that we would get together the next time I was in Chicago, and that we would bring Rachel and his girl, who would maybe be his wife by then.

Chapter Five

The flight back to the coast seemed to take forever. It was always that way when there was something important waiting on the other end. And Rachel was the most important thing in my life right now, perhaps ever. I could see her all dressed up standing next to me at the Justice of the Peace, more beautiful than ever.

There was no one to greet me at the airport. I had given Rachel my itinerary as far as flight times , so it seemed unusual to me that she wasn't there.

I took a yellow cab out to my home in La Jolla. There were no cars in the driveway, which wasn't really unusual. They were probably both in the garage. What really disturbed me was the absence of lights in the main house. With the two hour difference between Chicago and San Diego, it was only a little after nine. There should have been some activity. Rachel never went to bed before eleven.

I looked toward the guest house. It was dark too. I went to my front door, and then I saw it. A rope was stretched across the doorway from a sawhorse on either side of the entrance. In the middle was a sign that proclaimed POLICE-Do not enter.

I could feel a tightness beginning in my stomach, the same as I felt when we first boarded the rubber rafts for the journey to the hostile island during World War Two. It had quickly become a cramp that threatened to double me over in pain. It was the same thing I was experiencing when I saw the police sign. I imagined the worst, and with the picture of it in my mind, my world came crashing down. What if Rachel was dead?

I felt weak all over as I looked back toward the street. The cab was gone. I tried to gather my thoughts. Maybe there was a car in the garage. As I started in that direction I realized that even if I could get in there, I didn't have any keys. It wasn't likely that they were left in an ignition even if the cars were there.

In my mind at that point I only had one option left, short of screaming my head off in the middle of the very quiet street. I walked the nearly hundred yards to the nearest neighbor's house. Lucky for me they were still up. The people who lived there were pretty old and usually turned in early.

The husband took me to the La Jolla police station, and waited in his car, just in case I still needed transportation. I didn't even have the presence of mind to thank him.

The officer at the desk informed me that there had been a shooting at my place. He offered little information after that, except to say that the victim had been taken to Mercy hospital in the Hillcrest district of San Diego. Mercy was pretty well known as a trauma center, among other things. My stomach tightened a little more.

When I reached the floor I'd been directed to, I hoped Rachel would greet me in the hall. Instead it was Joe who saw me and came walking rapidly my way.

Before I could say anything, he blurted out, "We had no way to reach you in Chicago, or I would have called. Rachel's been shot!"

There, it was out. My worst fear had been realized. "Is she still alive?" I held my breath, waiting for his answer.

"She's in surgery now. It's been three hours since they wheeled her out, and I haven't heard anything yet."

I needed more answers than that, "What happened?"

"We might as well sit down", he said before continuing. "It had just gotten dark when I heard the shot. It seemed to have come from the big house. My first instinct was to run over there to check on Rachel, but I was afraid to go in there without a weapon. While I looked around for something I could use to defend myself I heard voices just outside. I couldn't make out what they were saying. It seemed to be two of them. Then I heard the sound of glass breaking, and I knew I was in trouble."

He paused to catch his breath before continuing, "I climbed up on the counter in the kitchen where I could reach the attic cover. I just had time to pull myself up, and slide the cover back on. They were there below me, searching for maybe five minutes before they left. When I heard the sound of a car starting I climbed down and ran over to check on Rachel. I found her in a pool of blood just inside the front door. She was still breathing. I pushed some towels from the kitchen against the wound, which was in her side, then I called the operator for an ambulance. They came within fifteen minutes. I had stopped the bleeding soon enough that she was still alive, but unconscious. I feel guilty that I didn't rush over to her earlier. Maybe it wouldn't have been so bad." He looked down at the floor, obviously feeling dejected about it.

"And maybe you would have been dead instead," I answered when he looked back up. "Did you get a look at them?"

"No. I just know that there were two of them."

Just then a nurse walked up to us. "She's out of surgery, but she can't see anyone for a while. Are either of you her husband?"

"No, but I'm her fiancé." I blurted, nervously.

"They were supposed to get married tomorrow," Joe said quickly, as if that made it better.

I was far away in my thoughts, back to that other time when we first met, and she'd been wounded. It couldn't have anything to do with that. That guy was put away for good. So why would anyone come after her? I had no answer for that question.

I was jerked back to the present when I saw a doctor coming toward us. "Are you relatives of Miss Embree?" he asked, with a concerned look on his bespectacled countenance.

I responded, "No, but I'm responsible for her. She has no one else in town. Her son is fighting in Korea."

"She lost a lot of blood", he continued. "Someone stopped the bleeding before she came to us, thank goodness. It probably saved her life."

"Then she's going to be okay?" I interrupted. "Yes young man," he was probably five years older than me, but that was all right. "But she lost a kidney. The bullet was lodged in the left one. It was too damaged to save. She will need a lot of bed rest. I'm assuming you'll stay with her?" He looked at me.

"Yes. I won't leave her side. When can I see her?" I asked, with a plaintive look on my face.

"She won't awaken for an hour or so. There's been a terrific jolt to her system. Why don't you go to the coffee shop on the ground floor, and come back about midnight."

I was surprised it was so late. Had I just returned to San Diego that evening? So much had happened, it seemed like it should be the next day.

"We'll do that Doctor, and thank you." I was extremely grateful at this juncture.

We remained in the coffee shop as suggested for over an hour. There was little conversation between Joe and I, but I did thank him profusely for saving my girl's life. He minimized his part in the nightmare, and again apologized for hiding, instead of running right to the big house. If he had done that, I was pretty sure he wouldn't have survived to help Rachel, and I told him so.

There's a surreal feeling when you see a loved one helpless-looking like Rachel was when I entered her hospital room. It's like it should be happening to someone else. She'd been so vital, so alive, not to mention beautiful beyond belief to me. Now as she lay there helpless, and pale-looking, it looked like she was just barely hanging on, and I had an impulse to check her pulse to see if she had passed away. Before I could act on it, her eyes opened. There was no sign of recognition, only something that looked like fear in them.

"How do you feel honey?" As soon as I said it I felt stupid. I wouldn't have been surprised if she had answered, 'How do you think I feel, you idiot?'

Instead she whispered, "I feel like I've been run over by a cement mixer." She tried a smile, but it didn't come off.

I bent down to kiss her on the cheek, but she stopped me with one word, "Don't".

"Do you want me to leave?" The words were hard to get out.

"Yes, I think you should," she answered. "I'm very tired."

As I started for the door she said, "I'm not the same person as when you left, Ivan. Please be patient with me."

"I will, baby. We have all the time in the world." I said it, but that's not what I felt. I was suddenly thinking life is short, and for some reason I was now on the outside looking in.

Chapter Six

Before I left the hospital I asked Joe to look after Rachel while I was gone. He assured me he would. He asked where I was going, but I was evasive. I wasn't sure what my next move would be.

I needed to get more information as to what happened at my house, but it was the middle of the night. I didn't think the police would have anything yet, and they wouldn't share it if they did. I should probably talk to Rachel again to get particulars, at least from her standpoint. Whether or not she would be receptive was the big question. She had seemed distant. It could be that she blamed me for what happened. I wasn't there with her, and maybe I should have been.

I suddenly realized that I hadn't even given her a ring. We'd been in such an all-fired hurry to tie the knot that the traditional rituals had been forgotten, at least by me.

I didn't know it but I was driving back to La Jolla while I was trying to figure everything out. It's a wonder I didn't hit something. One thing was for sure. I would need my gun.

I had a .44 handgun from when I worked in Intelligence with the Navy. I didn't ever want to use it, and I hadn't so far. It was tucked away in a drawer in my bedroom. I never looked at it in all the time since my discharge from the Marines.

I ignored the rope this time and used my key to enter through the front door. I retrieved the handgun and all the ammo I had, which was three clips. I hoped it was still good.

Suddenly I was very tired. I collapsed on my bed fully dressed, and was asleep in minutes.

I awoke when the Sun's light streamed through the bedroom window and hit me right in the face. Since I had already broken the law by even being in my house, I decided it wouldn't hurt to shower and shave, along with shedding my wrinkled clothes.

When I headed back to the hospital, some fifteen miles away, it was nearly ten. I didn't know when visiting hours were, but I should be close. I wondered if Joe had gotten any sleep.

As it was I couldn't get in to see Rachel until eleven, so I used the time to shop for an engagement ring. The one I picked out was not gaudy, but it had a small diamond. I hoped I would be back buying a wedding ring later that week.

I was optimistic that Rachel would be more receptive to my questioning than the night before. I really needed answers, and, to be honest, I wanted her to fall in my arms and prove that, at least with us, everything was all right. I was feeling guilty for having left her.

When I entered her room, Joe was there, and he was holding her hand. When he saw me he jumped up and came over to me with his right hand outstretched. I took it, and looked at Rachel.

"She's feeling good this morning." Joe said. I ignored him and stepped to her bedside. "Is that right sweetheart?"

"I do feel better, but I'm still hurting some." She attempted a smile, but it didn't quite come off. "Did you sleep here last night with Joe?" she continued.

"No. I had something to do at the house." I felt underneath my jacket. The gun was there, in a shoulder holster.

"I need some answers honey, but if you're not up to it yet just let me know."

"All right, but I don't remember much." She frowned slightly.

"Did you recognize the guy who shot you?"

She shifted a little under her covers, "No I'd never seen either of them before."

"So there were two of them?"

"Yes."

"Now comes the hard part. What did they look like?" I was hopeful when I asked. I needed something to go on.

"It all happened so fast. I opened the door, and they pushed their way in. Then the smallest of the two shot me. He didn't say anything." Then she thought of something else. "Before I passed out I heard them talking. The one who fired the gun had an accent,
European I think. That's all I remember until I woke up here after my surgery."

"That's great baby", I said.

"Oh wait, I do remember something else. The shooter's right ear was missing, or at least most of it was. I was so fixated on it that I didn't even notice that he had a gun. Does that help?"

I was shocked to hear about the ear. I knew who it was! I also knew I would have to return to Chicago.

"You've been great. I don't want to tire you anymore, so I'm going to get out of here." Then, almost as an afterthought I reached in my jacket pocket and produced the ring. I picked up Rachel's left hand as I said, "I should have given you this earlier. Please forgive me."

She looked at Joe who was standing by the door, glancing at the linoleum floor. As she pulled her hand back before I could slip the ring on her finger, she almost whispered, "I can't take your ring Ivan, at least not now.

So much has happened and I'm not sure of anything right now. Can I have some time to think about it?"

Chapter Seven

January in San Diego is beautiful, in its own way. The hills and surrounding mountains, which are usually barren and brown in the hot summers, have a tinge of green. The air, for the most part, is much clearer than in the heat of July and August, so the ocean and the bays, along with the rural lakes, seem much more blue. I read somewhere that San Diego has the most even climate in the world. The sixty plus degree afternoons at this time of year would seem to attest to that.

So why was I heading back to Chicago, and a bone-chilling winter? Rachel was out of danger. It was clear to me that she wasn't the target of the gunmen anyway. It was Joe they were after. The reason hadn't become apparent, but I knew I would find the shooter in the Windy City, and I had a score to settle with him. I had to get him before he came back after Joe, and he surely would. Whatever my amnesiac friend had on the killer or his employer, I didn't want Rachel to become trapped in the crossfire again.

It had been a long shot at best that August Schell would end up in Chicago, or even the United States for that matter. He should have died in his native Vienna, Austria in 1940. Augie, as he was known as a child, had been sent to stay with his father's brother in Marseille, France a few days before the Nazis stormed into their rural home and set the two elder Schells on fire. They had been gentle people; the father was a music teacher, and Augie's mother took in washing to make ends meet. The crime that sealed their fate in the eyes of the Nazis was that they were Jewish.

When told the news, which had reached the coastal French town a few weeks later, Augie didn't even cry for his parents, though he loved them deeply. The seventeen-year-old disappeared from his guardian's home the day after he heard what had happened. Soon afterward German soldiers, one at a time, began turning up dead near the French city. They were burned beyond recognition.

The young Austrian, who was often mistaken for a German, and protected by papers forged by a sympathetic printer, escaped detection until late 1942. His revenge had escalated by that time so that he was personally responsible for killing sixty of the enemy, five of them officers. It had not been possible to burn them all, so he just slit their throats, and watched while they died.

Finally the Bosch issued a proclamation, posted on nearly all lampposts from France to Berlin, and offering a large reward for information leading to the capture of one August Schell. Of course none of the locals would talk. To them the young killer was a hero. It had taken the Nazis quite a while to identify him. They restricted their soldier's movements in such a way that they were not allowed to walk anywhere on the streets alone.

No one gave him up, but he was spotted by a patrol on a street outside of Lion, France just after he had killed a woman German sympathizer, who would have turned him in. He was able to make it to the woods nearby and avoid capture. He found a cave, and quickly covered the entrance with brush. The enemy searched the area for days, but never found him.

Unfortunately the cave was the home of a wild dog, who didn't appreciate the intrusion. The animal attacked August, biting a huge chunk out of his right ear before he could get his hands around the dog's neck and strangle it to death. It gave him food and drink (if you can consider dog blood drink) for what would be a long stay in the cold, damp hideout. The dead animal's fur also helped keep him warm. The stench in the cave was almost enough to drive the fugitive out into the hands of the waiting enemy.

There was no news, good or bad, about the young resistance fighter from late 1942 until the liberation of France in 1944. In that year He was conscripted by the Allies and became a scout for the American infantry. Because of that Augie got an escorted pass to Berlin in 1945 and was in that city for what turned out to be VE day.

It was during the long march and its periodic battles that he met and became friendly with two American GIs; Christopher

Ellison and Aaron Small. The two men, who looked enough alike to be brothers, but were not related, took Augie under their wing. They had both been drafted out of Chicago, where they were small-time hoods, trying to work their way up the gangland ladder.

When the American troops returned to the States after VE day, August Schell, trained assassin, went with them.

It wasn't long before the young Austrian became an urban legend, with a string of killings that allowed Christopher Ellison and Aaron Small to ascend to a high position in Chicago's underworld. The police were bought off, so that charges were never brought, and all the slayings went unsolved.

Chapter Eight

When Robert Chase was assigned to the Chicago office of the FBI, he went reluctantly. He had fallen in love with Washington State and the Olympic peninsula where he and Carolyn, his wife of only two years had made their home. She was expecting their first child, so she didn't travel with him.

The thirty-five year old had been a confirmed bachelor before he met the woman who would completely change his thinking on the ball and chain life. Carolyn was a stunning blonde of five and a half feet. Her twenty-two inch waist complemented her rather large bosom well, and accentuated it.

She met Bob Chase by chance at a Thanksgiving party held at a mutual friend's home. She had a date, and he also was with another woman. She disliked him at first. He had had the nerve to leave his date in his car while he came inside to have a celebratory drink. He explained that the other woman didn't know anyone there and was extremely self-conscious. It was inexcusable to Carolyn that he would leave her in the car, it being late November and with the temperature near forty.

Later, when they kept running into each other at various parties, she began to think she had been hasty in her judgment. He was rather good looking. He stood just under six feet, which was nice considering how tall she was. His dark brown hair, with some premature graying tinges around the edges made him look distinguished. He looked like an athlete with his lithe one hundred and ninety pound frame. She was completely hooked by the time she found out what he did for a living.

The courtship progressed rapidly, and they were married in a small June wedding before a Justice of the peace. Their two best friends acted as witnesses. Bob was in the middle of a case, so their honeymoon consisted of one night at Ocean Shores where they had driven after one drink with their friends. Nevertheless they were deeply in love.

When he left for the Midwest, Bob told Carolyn that their forced separation would only be for a few months, and when she and the baby could travel they would be together again. She cried when he boarded the American Airlines plane, but there was nothing she could do to change things. The FBI's timing was incredibly bad.

In Chicago Robert Chase learned his assignment right away. He would be going undercover to infiltrate the mob, which was becoming extremely violent for the first time since Capone was put away for income tax evasion. Ever since prohibition was repealed the City had been reasonably quiet. There were still murders, but not on a scale experienced in the 20s and 30s. The gangsters had found a way to peacefully coexist. But now, for some reason, there was a new killing just about every week. The authorities needed to know why. They couldn't send in one of their own, because their faces were familiar to the locals. Enter Robert Chase. He was given a fake identity and background that identified him as a low-level hood from Detroit.

He began by frequenting the bars around the South side of town, acting tough and getting into brawls with the locals. He was picked up by the Chicago police, mugged and fingerprinted, then thrown in jail. He made it known that he wanted to become connected, and soon after being released for lack of a complaint, he was approached by a member of the organized crime family headed by Chris Ellison and Aaron Small and fronted by the Longshoreman's Union. He was in.

It wasn't long before he became an enforcer for the protection end of things. He, along with another gang member, was responsible for keeping revenue flowing into the gang's coffers from South side bar owners who were afraid not only of being raided by the cops for selling to minors or other trumped-up charges, but also of being burned out by the mob if they didn't pay up.

If things ran smooth in Bob's district, it was hoped that he would be able to get closer to the big guys, and build a case against them. It would be difficult, however, because the local police were playing ball and looking the other way, for a price. Local law enforcement didn't know about Robert Chase, who was known as Benny to the mob, except to think he was just another small time racketeer from Detroit.

Chase was able to make regular reports through an agent whom he met at a prearranged location once every week. He was moving up in the organization, and checked in regularly, until Christmas-time in 1951, when he stopped making reports and, as far as the FBI was concerned, disappeared completely from sight.

Chapter Nine

I had to figure out a way to keep Rachel safe when she came home. It wasn't likely that the trigger- happy gunman would be back, at least not for Rachel, but I couldn't risk it.

I could arrange for a rental to house Joe temporarily. That way maybe whoever wanted him dead wouldn't come back to the La Jolla place. It seemed like they knew our whereabouts somehow. I would also have to address that.

The leak had to be in Chicago. Anywhere else wouldn't make any sense. It had started there. In order to figure it out, I would have to return there. Meanwhile I was thinking I would hire a full-time bodyguard to protect Rachel. She wouldn't like it, but I would have to convince her. It would only be for a few days, hopefully.

When I arrived at the hospital I found Rachel alone in her room. "Hi" I said after entering.

She looked up and smiled, "Hello darling. I owe you an apology. I was not myself before."

"I didn't mind." I lied. "You were pretty doing it." It had really bothered me at the time. I was thinking, 'Am I really that insecure to think that there could be something between her and Joe?'

She took my hand as I sat next to her on the edge of her bed. "I wasn't really thinking rationally. I was mad that you had left me to be attacked again."

"I wanted to talk to you about that. I think the gunmen were after Joe for some reason. In fact I'm sure of it." I paused for a second before continuing, "so what I want to do is put Joe up in town, and hire a bodyguard to watch you."

She started to protest, but I stopped her. "I have to go back to Chicago to end this, whatever it is, and I won't just leave you alone, even though I think the attempted killers have gone back to their holes."

She couldn't argue with my logic, even though she might have wanted to. "Whatever you think is best. I trust you." Then she added, "But be careful. I don't want to lose you now." She squeezed my hand to emphasize her feelings.

"I wonder where Joe is?" I said, to change the subject. I had made my point and it looked as if she would go along with it. I didn't want to press my luck.

"I don't know," she answered. I haven't seen him since I awoke from my nap."

As if on cue, Joe opened the door and walked in.

"Where have you been?" I asked.

He smiled and answered, "I saw a shrink about my condition."

"And...?"

"I'm getting to that," he grinned. "The doc listened to my story. Then he examined

232

my head and my eyes. He thinks the amnesia is temporary, but he couldn't tell me how long it will last. There's only a slight chance in his mind that it's permanent. Of course this was kind of a snap judgment on his part. I'm going to go back in to see him in a couple of weeks."

"That sounds encouraging." I said.

All this time Rachel said nothing, but now she jumped in with "That's really good news Joe. I'll bet everything's going to be all right."

"Yeah, I think so. Thanks Rachel." He said, looking at her. "How are you doing?"

"I'm healing slowly, and I'm not feeling any pain, thank God. I've had enough of that."

I told Joe my plan. He said he wanted to go to Chicago with me, but I nixed that. "I don't think that's such a good idea. You'd be an easier target there. Let me do some digging around on my own first."

He had no choice but to agree, since he didn't have any money, and very few clothes.

I waited until Rachel was released from the hospital, and comfortable in my home, with the hired bodyguard ensconced outside the front door. The police had finished their forensic investigation the day before. Lab reports of fingerprints weren't in yet, but the cops shouldn't be bothering Rachel while I was gone. They'd already done all the interviewing they needed, at least for now.

It was a rainy windy day in Chicago when my plane landed. I decided to check into the same hotel as before and wait out the storm before following up on what I'd learned on my last trip. I rented a car at the airport and headed downtown. Once in my room I began to formulate a plan for the next day which was Wednesday.

I wanted to see my friend Jerry Greenway again. I had to rule him out as the leak who had fingered Joe, and got Rachel almost killed in the process. If he was clean as I suspected, he might be able to recall something that would help me in my investigation.

The sky outside my hotel window was gray, and with a steady rain tapping on the glass, I decided the weather wouldn't break for a while so I stretched out on the double bed to take a nap. It was just a few minutes later that I heard a knock on the door.

No one in the city should know I was there, but just in case I retrieved my gun from the holster I had hung up in the closet.

I looked through the peephole and saw the face of a man I didn't recognize, until I noticed he was missing most of the ear on his right side. My blood began to boil, thinking of my girl with a hole in her side, but I wasn't ready to confront August Schell yet, not until I learned the reason for the attack on Rachel and why they were so interested in silencing Joe permanently. I remained quiet until he gave up and left.

I had to be careful, but I needed to know where the gunman went. I got my jacket and holster. I was already dressed otherwise. I waited a few minutes before entering the hall, and heading for the stairs. It was only three flights down to the lobby.

When I reached the street I didn't see my quarry right away. I searched in both directions and was just about to give up, when I saw him. He was getting into a black Buick Roadmaster on the other side of the street, about a half-block away. I quickly walked to the parking lot to retrieve my rental car.

I was able to catch up to the vehicle I thought was Schell's about three blocks from where he started. He soon made a turn and started out toward the Lake. Just when I thought he might be heading out to the north, and maybe the park up there, he turned again. Before long I recognized the area. When he stopped it was right outside the Longshoreman's hall.

Chapter Ten

　　Chris Ellison's old man had been implicated in the St. Valentine's Day massacre. Whether or not he actually participated in the slaughter was never proved. But as a result of the publicity Eddie Ellison was elevated to a place of importance in the Chicago underworld.

　　He'd been a small-time player until late in 1929. He was mostly an enforcer for one of the lesser gangs of the area. When Al Capone was sent to prison, Ellison was able to assemble his own gang. It wasn't as big or powerful as Frank Nitti's bunch, but they did all right, and managed not to step on any of the big boy's toes.

　　To say that Chris had an ideal childhood would be the exact opposite of the truth. His father, when he was around, was merciless in his treatment of the boy whom he openly called a bastard. He whipped the child as early as age four, and when he couldn't find his belt, he used his fists.

　　Chris had no mother to soften his treatment. Rumor was she had been a one-night stand who was beaten to death by his father not long after her child was born.

　　The dark-haired, blue-eyed boy was only seven when his father was finally convicted of a relatively minor crime of extortion and sent to prison, where he died at the hands of another inmate. Chris spent the rest of his childhood in a Chicago home for boys.

He was constantly in trouble. It wasn't long after he turned twelve that the young tough had assembled his own gang in the home. The oldest kid there was fourteen and even he was afraid of Chris Ellison.

Before Chris was expelled from the school at the age of sixteen he met a little redheaded girl whose name was Sally Singleton. She was swept off her feet by the good-looking boy with the tough attitude. Sally was just a few months younger than him.

He was slightly awkward with her, since there had been no woman in his home in those early years. He had no sisters, thank God. For surely they wouldn't have been able to withstand the punishment the father handed out.

Chris had actually had two conquests by the time he met Sally. They had thrown themselves at him, and he'd just done what they had expected. This new girl was different though. She liked him right away, but she knew that, to be taken seriously, she would have to play hard to get.

At first Sally, who was fully developed, with a slim figure, acted as though he wasn't even there. Chris didn't know how to react to that, since he was very interested in her. She knew he lived in a boy's home, and that it was little more than a reform school. That just made him more interesting.

237

In order for him to take her out, he would either have to obtain permission from the headmaster at the home, or sneak out. He wasn't in the greatest standing there, because of his gang activities, so the second option would have to do.

They finally got together for a movie date when he snuck out for the evening, and she told him she would just go with him this once, but she had a boyfriend. It was stretching the truth, since she had broken up with the other boy when she became interested in Chris.

Of course he was caught, but not before their movie date. She was really nice to be with, and he was on his best behavior. Sally decided Chris was the one for her. But she would have to change him in such a way that he wouldn't have any more fights or get into trouble at all. Her parents would never allow her to see him if they thought he had a bad reputation. She had been brought up in a strict Catholic environment, and her parents were perhaps overly protective of their only child.

Chris's privileges were rescinded for a month. He would only be able to attend school, and would have to catch the school bus back to the home right after class. He wouldn't be able to do anything extra-curricular like sports. That part was okay with him. He thought that stuff was sissy-like anyway. Why would anyone want to work that hard when there was no payoff at the end?

Seeing Sally only at school was not the way Chris wanted to go. His hormones were raging, and he wanted to be with her alone. But it didn't happen for a while.

She was hurting too. She didn't understand what was occurring inside her body. She never had a physical problem with any of the other boys she had been with. She just told them no, and pushed them away when they became aggressive. But Chris was different. She wanted him to touch her, and not to stop. She wanted to be as close to him as physically possible.

It finally happened that they could be together. She told her parents she was going to a movie with girlfriends, and since he had been on his best behavior for a while, he was able to get a pass for the evening, provided he was back by ten P.M.

They found a spot that was secluded in the woods nearby. Neither of them had a blanket, but they were out of control with desire and fell together on a grassy spot near a large oak tree.

Chris tried to be gentle after removing his shirt. He really cared for this lovely girl beneath him. He reached behind her back and tried to unfasten her brassiere but it was fighting him. Sally stopped him, and he was sure he had gone too fast with her. She reached behind her back and found the hooks that held the supporting garment. Suddenly there was nothing between them but their own supple skin. Both bodies were pale from lack of sunshine.

239

As he entered her, she moaned in pain. He tried to pull away. He felt so much for her that he didn't want to hurt her. She again stopped him. "It doesn't hurt now."

There was a sticky liquid on his leg, and when he looked down he realized it was blood. He was worried, but she held him tight against her, and her moaning now was obviously with pleasure. "I love you, Sally," he blurted, louder than the surroundings called for. He quickly looked around to see if anyone had heard.

"Oh Chris, I love you too." She responded, pressing even closer to him.

The pleasure was so intense for him that he exploded with a delicious feeling that, although it didn't last long, was the best experience he ever had.

She seemed content to just lie there with them holding each other, even though he was sure she didn't feel what he did. He had wanted to yell out with pleasure. The only thing that stopped him was being out in the open the way they were.

They weren't able to get away often during the next year, but their emotions remained strong for each other. It was good fortune that she didn't become impregnated. Contradictory to her religious upbringing, she used protection. When it became apparent to Sally that she would let Chris make love to her, she visited a doctor other than the family physician, and was fitted for a diaphragm. Chris himself was unaware of Sally's precautions. Minimizing the chances of pregnancy was not something he even thought

240

of. It worked out well because neither of them would have been ready for the responsibility of a child.

Chapter Eleven

It would make a nice story to say that Chris and Sally lived happily ever after, and that he straightened out to be a pillar of the community, but that would be far from accurate.

Before Chris turned sixteen and was kicked out of the home, a new kid arrived. Aaron Small was already a hardened criminal by the time the state of Illinois got him. He was still a minor, so he avoided prison. The state reform school was filled to capacity so Aaron lucked out and was sent to the home where Chris held sway as the head tough.

It was inevitable that the two would lock horns. It was fortunate that the clash was impromptu, so neither boy was armed.

Aaron had not even spent a full day at the home, when he tried to assert himself on the general population. All the boys ate at the same time in a fairly large hall. They stood in line waiting their turn at the food table. Some of the boys, who had been allowed to eat earlier, were the servers. They were rotated from day to day so that all got their chance to do it. Chris was near the end of the line, when he saw Aaron push his way in near the food table. He decided to let it go this time, and talk to the new boy later when no one was around.

That no longer became an option when he saw the new guy, who was fairly large in comparison to most of the younger residents, and even some who were his own age, grab onto the shirt of the first server, a boy of 13. Apparently he hadn't been given enough of the meat to satisfy him.

Chris, the self-appointed leader in the school, felt obligated to protect the other boys. He raced toward the food tables, grabbed the back collar of Aaron's loose-fitting, school issued gray shirt, and yanked him backward violently. The new boy fell hard onto his backside. Chris didn't stop there. He pulled Aaron back toward the end of the line, with his right hand still firmly grasping the other boy's collar, and his left tugging at his belt.

Aaron Small, though flailing wildly with his own arms could do nothing to stop the humiliation.

"This is where you belong," Chris shouted when they reached the back of the line, "You'll wait your turn if you know what's good for you!"

When he was released, Aaron Small made a hasty retreat from the dining room without a word. Chris Ellison had won the first skirmish, but there would be others.

Not long afterward, when the two nearly grown boys were alone, Chris tried to talk to Aaron to smooth things over. They would have to coexist in small surroundings for nearly a year before each would be free to make his own way. They encountered each other in a vestibule that served as a library for the boys.

"I wanted to get some time to talk to you," Chris opened.

Aaron stared at the other boy, who was about the same size. "Yeah, what do you want?"

Chris was sizing him up while he spoke. He had blue eyes too and, though he parted it differently their hair was nearly the same color, with Aaron's just a shade lighter. They could almost be mistaken for brothers. "We don't need to be enemies," he began.

"Well we are," Aaron interrupted. "You started it at dinner that night," and he added, "but I'm going to finish it."

"I can see why you might feel that way, after the way I treated you, but I want to make it up to you."

"And just how would you do that?"

Chris had thought this next thing over, "I can cut you in on stuff we all do together."

"Yeah, like what?" Aaron didn't want to show too much interest, but he had heard things from the other kids; about how they had a smooth operation going to get money, cash he would need when he broke away from this place.

"You'll find out soon enough. Is it a deal?" Chris answered.

Aaron reluctantly agreed, and that was the beginning of a fragile peace between them. What could be called friendship came a few weeks later, and was as surprising to one as to the other.

Sally Singleton was to meet Chris on the edge of their neighborhood in South Chicago on a cool night in December of 1939. There was a wooded area there that the two lovers used for their rendezvous once in a while. Sally was early, probably because she hadn't seen her boyfriend for a week, since school let out for the Christmas holiday. He'd said he had chores at the home, but what really prevented their getting together was that he and his gang were breaking into stores, and stealing goods that were to be presents for others. Chris had a fence, so to speak, who would give them cash for the merchandise.

While Sally waited, a few local boys saw her. One of them was her previous boyfriend, whom she had broken up with to be with Chris. He still held a grudge, and this night, with liquor flowing through his loins, and lusty thoughts swirling through his brain, he was going to get even.

When the spurned kid grabbed Sally, with his buddies gathered around, he began pulling her toward the darkness of the nearby trees.

She screamed, but the only one close enough to hear her was Aaron Small, who had just rounded a corner not far away.

He rushed to the scene, and with a pocket knife he carried while away from the home, he slashed the first boy he came to in the arm. Before the scream of pain left his lips, Aaron was on a second spectator. He plunged the knife deep into the kid's abdomen. In doing so he got the attention of Sally's

245

attacker, who jumped on Aaron's back, trying to pull him down. Were it not for Chris's arrival on the scene, Aaron himself would have been in serious trouble. After pulling the one boy off Aaron, the two of them quickly dispatched the others, using their fists this time because the knife had been dropped in the struggle.

All the aggressors ran off, one holding his bloody arm, and another holding his stomach. The confrontation was over in less than five minutes.

Sally rushed into Chris's arms, and then turned to thank her savior Aaron Small. From then on the two teenage boys were almost constant companions.

Chapter Twelve

I had to get my mind around this. The mystery guy who lived in the mansion by the park disappeared into the union hall. August Schell also went there. That place had to be the key. Joe's only clue to his identity had been that tattered piece of paper with the San Diego Longshoremen's Union hall address on it. 'And don't forget' I told myself, 'Jerry Greenway might be involved in this too'. I had to rule him out before anything else. I liked Jerry. Hell, I owed him my life. All this was bouncing around in my head as I found my way back to my hotel.

There was a message waiting for me at the desk when I got there. It was from Rachel. I was supposed to call her.

She answered on the first ring. "Hello?" Her voice was melodic, at least to me.

"You rang, my love?" It had been a long time since I had been able to call anyone my love. It felt good.

"I just wanted to hear your voice." She sounded wistful. "Have you been able to find out anything about Joe?"

"Not really," I answered. "I've got a few leads that I want to check out, but nothing concrete. Has Joe remembered anything?"

"Not that he's told me. He called a while ago to see how I was doing. He's really sweet."

"Just remember, I'm sweeter, and I don't mind if he's chocolate candy from a distance. You're my girl."

"I do believe you're jealous. I'm flattered." She replied.

"Seriously kid, he's a good looking guy and he's there. I'm not. I'm just looking after my interests."

Her voice took on a somber tone, "You have nothing to worry about in that regard. I'm hopelessly in love with you." And then she said, teasing, "I just wish I wouldn't keep getting shot when I'm with you."

"I'm going to put an end to that, I promise you."
I never meant anything more in my life.

We talked of banalities for another half hour before closing with "I love you." It was nice hearing her voice, but it just added to the longing I felt for her. It was like I had two lives; a normal one when I was around her, and the violent one I chose for my career.

Back to the work at hand. I called Jerry Greenway. He had just come home to his apartment from a day's work on the docks of Lake Michigan. We arranged to meet at the same saloon as before. He needed time to shower, so we set a time of six-thirty to get together.

He was already at a booth when I arrived. "Hi," he greeted me in a cheerful tone. We shook hands.

248

"I thought maybe you would have your wife with you?" He questioned.

I looked at him. He seemed innocent enough. "No. It's a long story. We're on hold for awhile. How about you? Are you a married guy?"

"No. Not yet, but we set a date for June. It'll be torture until then, but she's a traditional gal. She doesn't have any folks, just a brother. Anyway, that will give me time to raise the money for a big wedding. I'll send you an invite." It sounded like he meant it.

"I'll be there," I answered. Silently I thought, 'if I'm still alive.' I would have to go up against August Schell at some point. I had a score to settle with the hired assassin.

"Do you remember that I told you about my place in La Jolla?" I had to get into this at some point.

"Sure I do. You said your Rachel was living there with you, and the guy with amnesia too."

He was so forthcoming he couldn't be the leak. "Did you tell anyone else?" It was the sixty-four dollar question.

He didn't answer right away. "Let me think. "I told Judy, my fiancée, and I might have mentioned it to Manny, at the hall, while I was waiting for work. Why?"

I wasn't ready to share what happened with him just yet. "I'll tell you sometime. Let's just enjoy our drinks." I picked up my Manhattan to emphasize the point.

"Okay," he said, lifting his beer, "but I'm really curious."

249

It was nearly midnight, and three Manhattans later that I headed back to my room. I was convinced that Jerry was clean, and that Manny was the link to the attempt on Rachel's life. I would see him tomorrow. Except for the booze I had consumed, I probably wouldn't have gotten much sleep, but as it was I slept soundly until I was awakened by the maid, inquiring if she could clean my room.

Chapter Thirteen

I was in the middle of a recurring dream, sometime in the middle of the night, when I heard a loud rapping sound. I was confused. It didn't belong in my dream, unless it was from a repeating rifle. I was in the thick underbrush of a Japanese-held jungle, and I was alone. I looked out toward the sea, and I saw a lone submarine. Suddenly It blew up, sending tiny pieces of shrapnel over my hideout.

I heard the rat-tat-a-tat again. This time it sounded like a loud drum beat. That really didn't fit. Then I heard a voice. It was a woman's voice. "Ivan, are you in there?"

I was awake now. The sound I had heard must have been knocking. I looked at the clock by my bedside. It seemed to read four-fifteen. In my dazed mind, I said to no one in particular, "This is a strange time for visitors."

"Please open the door darling, if you're there." It was Rachel's voice.

I was wide awake now. "Just a minute," I said, louder than I needed to. I sleep in the raw, so I pulled on a pair of slacks, and went to the door shirtless.

As I pulled it open, and I saw her standing there, she whispered, "Don't scold me darling, I just had to see you." And then she rushed into my arms, and buried her face in my shoulder.

"It's all right baby. I'm glad to see you too." Before I could say more she kissed me hard on the mouth, and pressed her entire body against mine.

I was never any good at reading women, but this time I figured it out. We moved together toward the bed, our lips and everything else still pressed together. She was wearing a loose-fitting blouse that buttoned in the front. I slid both my hands under her garment in the back, and fumbled with her brassiere hooks. She stopped me. "Wait," she said softly, and put her own arms behind her back. She worked to free herself while I turned my attention to the small buttons in the front. It was a tie, as I removed her blouse and the white brassiere fell to the floor.

"God you're beautiful," I stammered as I looked at her full breasts, which were more of a creamy color compared to her California-tanned shoulders.

She said nothing, and we both fumbled with the rest of our clothes before falling together on the soft bed sheets, that were still warm from my body heat.

I stopped, and lifting my head from her firm breast said, "Are you sure you're ready for this?"

"I've never been so sure of anything in my life," she answered and pulled me back down to her.

In that moment, there was nothing that would take me away from her. Anything I

252

had planned for the day would surely wait until the next. I was lost inside the warmth of her. This was how it was supposed to be. The act itself meant nothing. It was the love of one person for another that made it the most important and intense feeling on the planet. The pleasure was shared on many levels, only one being the nerve-tingling of physical release that was felt throughout our bodies.

As we fell away from one another, we both knew it would happen again. How soon it happened surprised even me. We were in the throes of a second orgasm only minutes after we coupled again, and the Sun still hadn't risen in the February sky. The darkness suited me just fine.

"I never knew it could be like this," Rachel whispered in her husky voice just before we stopped for breakfast. Neither of us was hungry, but it was a break our bodies needed.

We ordered in, holding each other until room service knocked on the door. I dressed completely before answering, to protect my lady's reputation.

Rachel had taken the red-eye flight to get to Chicago, and her weariness was beginning to show, so I let her sleep, holding her, with my eyes taking in the loveliness of her the whole time. Joe's amnesia and the attempt on Rachel's life, the whole reason for my being in the Windy city, was forgotten in the aftermath of what was turning out to be the best day of my life.

My confrontation with the killer August Schell, and the planners behind the attack in La Jolla, could wait until the next day. My gun could remain holstered for a little while longer, but not forever. I would always remember how close I came to losing the angel beside me. I would somehow find a way to take my revenge.

Chapter Fourteen

Having Rachel with me, though extremely pleasant, complicated things. August Schell had already paid a visit to my hotel room. I couldn't chance leaving her at his mercy if he should choose to come back.

She wasn't going to leave, and I didn't want her to. Using an outside line I had her call the hotel desk and arrange for another room using a fictitious name. It would accommodate two people. Later that afternoon she took her one suitcase and registered under the name of Mister and Mrs. Larry Evans.

I kept my original room, just in case, but I packed up my stuff and moved it into her room which was three floors up. I didn't want to be shuffling back and forth while she was there. I didn't use the elevator lest I be too conspicuous. Luckily it only took me two trips to complete the transfer.

I took my girl to a nice restaurant I'd been to with my ex-wife Annie. We ate Chateau Briand under candlelight, gazing into one another's eyes like newlywed youngsters, even though we were both on the other side of forty. We held hands waiting for the dessert. I was still enjoying the day, and didn't especially want it to end. I got the feeling she felt the same.

The hotel room door had hardly closed behind us when we clutched at each other again. "I had a lovely evening, my love," She said, breaking away from our lingering kiss just long enough to acknowledge how she felt.

"You're too beautiful for words," I answered as I steered her toward the bed.

"Are you sure you won't tire of me?" She barely had time to get the words out before I kissed her mouth again, and let my lips wander to her shoulder.

"What do you think?" I mumbled as my target moved lower, much lower.

She moaned appreciatively and said the words we'd both felt ever since she crossed the threshold of my previous room, "I love you so much!"

The thought crossed my mind that Rachel was a nymphomaniac, but only for a second. It wouldn't have mattered anyway. She was a perfect fit, in every way. We finally fell asleep around one the next morning, exhausted but happy.

She awoke before me. I reached for her in the bed, still only half awake. Not finding her I sat up quickly, looking around the small room. She wasn't there. I had what could be considered a panic attack, and jumped out of bed, looking for my clothes. Just then Rachel emerged from the bathroom, with a towel wrapped around her.

"Good morning, my darling," she said, with a smile on her face. "Did you sleep well?"

"What do you think?" I answered. "You wore me out." And I added, "You scared me too, when you weren't next to me when I woke up."

"I really needed a shower. I left some hot water for you, if you're ready."

"That sounds good, unless you want to climb back in bed with me?" I made it a hopeful question.

"I do, but I won't." She said, and walked over to me and took my hand. "I'm thinking we'll have the rest of our lives to explore each other. I hope that's not too crude a way to put it." She grinned.

"Nothing you do is crude, just cute." I said it in a playful way.

"So what do you have planned for today?" She changed the subject.

"I'm going to confront the guy I think fingered me to a killer. If I'm right he may lead me to the people who sanctioned the hit, which was supposed to be on Joe."

"Do you really have to do it?" She looked in my eyes and continued, "Joe doesn't really mean anything to you."

"No. You're right. He doesn't. But the gunman shot you. That makes it extremely personal." I answered. "I can't take a chance that you won't be a target again. These people, whoever they are, are ruthless."

After my shower I gathered up my clothes, and returned to the bathroom. Rachel smiled and said, "You can dress out here. I've seen you before."

"You're right," I answered, and dropped the towel.

Chapter Fifteen

Leaving Rachel was not the easiest thing I've ever done, but by mid-afternoon I was able to tear myself away. I made a mental note to talk to her about going back to San Diego. I wanted to keep her as far out of harm's way as possible.

I was about five minutes into my drive downtown, when I spotted it. I'd had to make a few turns, and this blue Oldsmobile stayed right with me. I could see two men in the car through my rear-view mirror. Traffic was so light that time of the day that I felt losing them would be impossible. I reached under my jacket for my shoulder holster, and I was relieved that I had remembered to strap it on. The forty-four had a calming effect on me. I was ready for trouble.

I had an easy time finding a parking place near the union hall, and as I walked the short distance I noticed the Olds parked just across the street. It was still occupied. I shrugged and walked into the shop.

I was right about it being a good time of day to confront Manny. He was there sitting at his desk, and no one else was in the hall. As I walked toward him, he looked up to see me and said, "Oh no, not you again. Don't you ever give up?"

I said nothing. I reached across the desk and pulled him to me. "What the hell," he muttered.

"You're going to tell me everything you know about the attack on my girl in San Diego, and you'd better do it fast." I shoved him against an adjacent wall for effect.

"You're crazy! I don't know what you're talking about."

"One more chance," I growled, and I pulled my gun out to show that I meant business.

"Honest fella, I don't know nothing." He was shaking so bad he almost had me convinced.

I took a different tack. "Who uses that back room?"

He answered quickly this time, "some of the bigwigs of the union. They have meetings here once in a while.

"What are their names?" And as an afterthought I said, "Where can I find them?"

"The only one I know the name of is Chris Ellison. He has something to do with the Longshoremen's union but I don't know what. Now will you let me go?"

I put my gun back in its holster and released the little guy, convinced that he would have told me what I needed to know if he could.

When I walked out of the office, the two men who were in the car parked across the street exited the vehicle. They crossed toward me. I recognized one as the earless hood August Schell. The other guy I didn't know.

He was reasonably tall, and looked like he was carrying. He wore a hat, but Schell didn't.

Just when I thought this would be the inevitable showdown, a police car rounded the nearest corner, and stopped right next to me. Schell and his partner turned around and walked back to their car.

A big, burly cop came up to me and said, loud enough to be heard a block away. "Face the car, and put your hands against the vehicle. Spread your legs." For effect he slapped my backside with his nightstick.
He quickly found my gun and removed it from its harness.

"Do you have a permit for this?" He growled.

I replied, "yes. It's on file with you guys. I'm a private investigator. What's this all about?"

The big one didn't answer, and his partner just stood nearby, looking amused.

They put me in their police car in the back seat. Soon we were at the police station. Once inside, the big one told the guy behind the counter, "Book him on assault with a deadly weapon."

"You've got to be kidding." I barely got it out before the big guy let me have it in the stomach with his nightstick.

"We'll let you know when you can talk. Otherwise keep your mouth zipped." He said.

I was photographed and fingerprinted after being relieved of the contents of my pockets. I was then led to a cell with a cot and commode. Of course it was Friday, and I would have to wait until Monday to see a judge, even if I could arrange bail somehow. It wasn't a question of money. I just had to find a lawyer who would set it up. I thought about Jeremy Taylor, but I didn't know how to reach him. He was the lawyer who brought me the case that in a roundabout way made me rich.

I couldn't see any other way not to bring Rachel into it. Then I remembered Jerry Greenway. The kid might do it. When I was given the chance I called the number he had given me. A woman answered, "Hello?"
It had to be his girl, what was her name? Judy. That was it.

"I'm Ivan Dunn. Is Jerry there?"

There was a pause of about three seconds before she answered. "Yes. I'll get him." I was relieved. I don't know what I would have done if he wasn't there. I only got one call.

"Hi Ivan," he greeted when he finally answered. "What's up?"

"It's a long story Jerry, but I'm in jail, and I need someone to arrange bail. I'll have to stay the weekend as it is. I go up before the judge first thing Monday morning. Can you handle it?"

He had sense enough not to question me then, and replied, "Sure. I'll take care of it. What precinct are you in?"

"It's the one downtown by the union hall."

"I'll be right there first thing Monday morning."

"I'm forever in your debt. One more thing, will you call my girl Rachel for me? She's at the hotel here in town." I gave him the number. Luckily I remembered it. I almost forgot to give him the name she was using. "Thanks Jerry."

He was sitting in the courtroom when I was led in. He paid the bail, and I was released. As we walked out onto the frozen street I asked him, "Did you get hold of Rachel?" When he nodded in the affirmative I continued, "Do you know where the union offices are? I think they're downtown somewhere."

"Yeah I think they are on Bell Street. I've only been there once, though." Jerry was being very helpful.

"Let me buy you a drink, kid, it's the least I can do to show my appreciation."

Jerry thought for a minute then said, "I think I can spare the time for one."

"I'm dying of curiosity Sarge. What the hell is going on?" Jerry asked after we found a table. "Why were you in jail?"

I told him about Rachel being shot, and Joe having amnesia, after apparently having been thrown in the lake to drown. I laid out my reason for having attacked his friend Manny. I also alerted him to the fact that August Schell had a reputation as a hired killer, and that he was associated with the Longshoremen's union somehow. Someone had led the killers to my home in La Jolla. I just didn't know who.

"Damn!" He exclaimed. "I had no idea you were going through all this."

I suddenly remembered Rachel was waiting for me at the hotel. "I've got to go Jerry," I said as I threw money for the drinks on the table. "I'll keep in touch, and thanks again."

Chapter Sixteen

Having grown up in Chicago I'd heard all the stories about Aaron Small, and I wasn't anxious to cross paths with him. Ask anyone who knew him even remotely and they would describe him as a good-looking blue-eyed devil with a violent temper, or words to that effect.

Rumor had it that his father had hanged himself rather than endure the constant harassment of the man's wife. The old man had been a mild-mannered haberdasher who was forced to marry a younger woman whom he had deflowered. The result was a six pound baby boy whom they named Aaron, because the mother liked the name. Aaron's father would never argue with his wife. She was larger than him, and stronger, of big-boned Norwegian stock. Neighbors of theirs, in a poor neighborhood on the south side of Chicago would tell of hearing them fight. Hers was the loudest voice. He often showed up at work with cuts and bruises on his face where she supposedly had hit him.

It was surprising that together they produced another offspring, a girl. There was no way the Smalls could handle bringing up another child in that environment. With prodding from the State, she was adopted out when she was three months old. Aaron had taken to the little baby, and was crushed when she was taken away. He vowed to find her someday.

Finally Aaron's father could take no more physical and mental abuse, and one day in the back room of his shop, he climbed on a chair, tied a rope to a beam, and with the other end fashioned into a noose around his neck, he jumped.

Aaron was seven years old when he wandered into his father's shop, and found the man, still swinging from the rope.

He couldn't go home after that. He was found a day later panhandling on a street corner for food money. He cried, and threatened to run away again if he was returned to his mother. The police were sympathetic, but their hands were tied. The law would not let them do anything other than send him back.

With no husband with whom to take out her anger, she transferred her wrath to the boy, beating him at the slightest provocation.

Aaron himself became a bully at school after a growth spurt that placed him above many of the other boys physically. By the time he was sixteen, the authorities had had enough, and he was transferred to the boy's home where he met Chris Ellison. His mother had pleaded with the court to release her from her guardianship of such an unruly boy.

By the time Aaron Small reached puberty he despised all females, young and old, except his sister. He stared at every young female he thought to be about her age, looking for similarities that might identify her, but to no avail. She seemed to be lost to him forever.

Since he couldn't stand to be around other girls his age, he masturbated almost daily to relieve the sexual stress he felt. He searched through paperback novels to find inspiration. In his mixed up mind he thought of the act as a punishment for girls.

His defense of Sally Singleton was just a reaction on his part to mix it up with the boys involved. He had no thought of her at all.

He finally visited a house of prostitution in Chicago's red-light district, to show that he was no homo, as some around him had come to suspect. After having his way with a slightly obese whore in her forties, he beat her so badly that she required hospitalization. No complaint was ever filed, because the whorehouse couldn't stand the publicity.

As luck would have it, both Aaron Small and Chris Ellison's draft number came up in the fall of 1943.
Neither of them had any felonies on their record yet, so they were classified 1-A. They attended boot camp together, and early in 1944 were shipped to England, near the English Channel. Their training continued in the months leading up to D-Day and they were in the assault force storming Omaha Beach on June the sixth.

Both men were very patriotic, surprisingly. They could never have ascended to positions of power in any other country, and they knew it. They were ready to fight for freedom. They were ferocious combatants.

266

Aaron volunteered for a one-man reconnaissance mission behind German lines. His expertise in street fighting and especially with a knife stood him in good stead one dark night when he encountered a patrol of six enemy soldiers. He couldn't know that they were young recruits, with none over seventeen years of age, save their sergeant. In the blackness he killed them one by one using only his knife to their throat, and picking off the trailing soldier first each time so they wouldn't rush him. The only sound was a gurgling noise. He shot the last two, including their leader, and then ran off to distance himself from the noise.

He received a commendation medal with a ribbon for the action. He proudly displayed it in the union office after the war.

Chapter Seventeen

So now I had a date with the Chicago superior court hanging over my head. Just what I needed. My stupidity amazes me sometimes. About the least that would come of it, I would have my license to carry a gun suspended. Luckily my next court appearance wouldn't be for a month and a half. Hopefully my business in the great state of Illinois would be concluded by then and Rachel and I could get on with our lives, together I hoped.

She was a little upset that I had landed in jail on what was to be a promising weekend for the two of us. But that's okay. So was I. I vowed to make it up to her. The flowers I brought home did ease her anger somewhat. I was never much of a flower man myself. It just seemed pointless because they all wilted and died. This situation required a bit of sacrifice on my part though, and the assorted bouquet did the trick.

"We've known each other such a short while, and already you know how to get to me, you scoundrel," She said, as she set the flowers on a nearby desk.

"They're pretty aren't they?" I lied. But they did smell good.

She took my hand, "what happens next with the law?"

"I'll go to court in a few weeks, and they'll probably reduce it to a misdemeanor, since I do have a permit for the gun. I'll pay a fine and that will be the end of it." I simplified it a bit, but she didn't need to worry about some stupid thing I did.

"Then will we go back to La Jolla?" she said, hopefully.

"We need to talk about that." I replied. "I think you should go back now."

She started to refuse, "But I want to stay here with you!"

"I know kid, but you might be in danger here. The hoods who want Joe dead are here, I'm sure of it, and I want you out of harm's way."

"Then come with me, please." She pleaded.

"I can't right now. There's always the chance they'll come back after us, and we can't live like that." I answered.

"Maybe you're right, but why put yourself in danger now?"

"It's just a question of now or later, and I'd rather get it over with." It made sense to me. Neither of us would sleep well with the threat of peril looming.

I called and made a reservation for Rachel to fly back to the coast. The first vacancy was two days off. I didn't like it but there was no other choice. It was too far to take a bus.

"I really don't think it's a good idea for you to leave the room until your flight."

She opened her mouth to object, but I stopped her. "It's just too dangerous with that lunatic Schell on the loose, and god knows how many others are after us. I wouldn't leave either, but I have a few leads I want to follow up on."

She didn't answer, probably figuring it wouldn't do any good, as hard-headed as I am. She was right. I picked up the phone.

"Who are you calling?" she was curious.

"The post office," I replied. "I have an idea on how to find out who lives in the big house by the lake park. There was no name on the mailbox, but if I can intercept some of the mail for that address, I can get a name."

Rachel looked at me. "And how do you hope to do that?"

"If I can find out when mail is delivered out there, I can be there get a look at the addressee on an envelope."

"Ingenious. And who's going to bail you out of federal jail when you're caught stealing mail?"

"I'm not going to take anything, just get a name." I thought it was a good idea.

I dialed the number from the phone book in our room. The clerk was very helpful, after I lied that I was new to the area, and expecting an important letter. Since I would be at work I needed to know when I should drive out and pick up my mail.

After a good night's sleep for the first time since I'd been incarcerated, I headed out to the lake, after kissing my lady goodbye.

I parked my rental vehicle on the street at the park and waited. I could see the mailbox of the big house to the north. I must have been sitting there for an hour when the mailman walked by my car on his way toward my target.

After he disappeared from sight I wandered in that direction, looking into the park to see if anyone noticed me. There was only one fisherman down by the water, and a couple paying attention only to each other by a big oak tree.

I reached into the mailbox and smiled. I was in luck. There were two envelopes inside. I pulled them out and looked at them, one at a time. They both were addressed to a Chris Ellison. One was sent from the Longshoreman's union, and the other listed no sender.

I quickly put both envelopes back into the mailbox and started back to my car. A man, dressed in black, emerged from the big house, saw me, and began yelling "Stop!".

I raised my arms, palm out, to show that I didn't take anything, and then I ran quickly to my car with the man from the house in hot pursuit. Thank God I was a little faster. He was only a few feet from my vehicle when I pulled away.

I was pretty sure it was the butler who saw me. I hoped he didn't recognize me, or I would most likely have another visit from the law. My stomach was still sore from the last time.

Chapter Eighteen

So Chris Ellison was probably the one in the overcoat I had seen entering the union hall. Maybe Joe was Aaron Small. I'd seen no evidence of his infamous temper, but he could be. Maybe the rap on his head had changed his persona too. I wasn't sure that could happen. I wish I knew a shrink in town I could talk to. There was a definite connection to the Longshoreman's union. They sent him mail.

I decided my next stop should be the office of the union that Jerry had said was downtown. I dropped by a phone booth and checked on the address. Before long I was parked in a lot only a block away. Street parking in the city was almost nonexistent during business hours.

I took an elevator to the third floor where the office was located. The sign on the glass door said simply, 'Longshoreman's Union'.

A pretty thing behind a cluttered desk asked, "Can I help you?"

Up 'till then I had no idea what I would say when I got there. I studied the voice. She had long flowing brown hair that seemed to me to be a World War Two style. She wore a one piece brown dress with a white collar. I couldn't see her shoes behind the desk, but I would have bet she wore patent leather with heels.

"I came to see Mr. Ellison. My name is Ivan Dunn." I waited for a reaction. There was none.

"Won't you take a seat Mr. Dunnopolous?" She said, as she waved to a bank of chairs against a far wall.

Okay, I was shook up. How did this woman know my full name? Only one person in town could have told her. I looked down at her nameplate. It read 'Judy Evanson'. She had to be Jerry Greenway's girlfriend.

I tested her. "How's Jerry?"

She turned red, and didn't speak for a second. She regained her composure and uttered, "I'm sure Mister Ellison will see you soon. Please be seated."

I knew one person I owed an apology to, but I didn't think that guy Manny would accept. I wondered how involved Judy was in all this. I hoped silently that she wasn't, and telling the boss was just an innocent slip.

From the time she got on the intercom to announce my presence, until I looked up at the clock on the wall behind her desk, it had been ten minutes. The door to the inner office had never opened. The second time I checked, twenty five minutes had elapsed.

I looked at Judy Evanson, and I could swear she had a smirk on her face. It was becoming evident that I would not get a look at Ellison that day, so I rose and walked out of there without so much as an 'I'll be back'.

When I stepped out of the elevator on the ground floor I saw two uniformed cops coming through the main entrance. I recognized one of them as the guy who exercised his nightstick in my gut.

I was sure they hadn't seen me as I moved out of their range of vision. I had the distinct feeling they were there to intercept me, for what reason I wasn't sure. I was out on bail, so I had to be careful.

After the cops disappeared into the elevator and its door had closed, I made my way out onto the snow-covered street. It hit me that this was one of the reasons I had moved west. The first snow was pretty, but it got dirty very fast, and ugly to drive in, even on level streets, let alone trying to navigate hills. Even if you were a good driver in the white stuff, you had to worry about the other idiots on the road.

I had to decide whether to tell Jerry about his girlfriend. I wondered if he knew she worked in the union office. He hadn't said anything about her being there.

Traffic was light as you might imagine with the snow. It wasn't late enough for rush hour, even in a city as large as Chicago.

I was halfway to Jerry's place when I noticed a tail. It was the same car as before. I couldn't do much about it, since the cops had confiscated my gun. I'd just have to wait to see how it played out. I didn't think I could outrun them.

When I reached my friend's house I quickly found a parking spot, and went to his door, turning back toward the street in time to see my shadow passing by. I could make out two men in the front seat. It didn't look as if the back was occupied. I couldn't make out the driver's face, but his passenger was clearly visible. I didn't know him.

When Jerry came to the door, I had already decided not to mention the Evanson girl. It would serve no purpose at this point. My friend was clean, I was sure of it.

"Hi. What have you been up to?" He questioned.

"I went out to the house by the lake park. I wanted to find out who lives there." I answered.

"Did you find what you were looking for?" He motioned me inside.

"The place belongs to Chris Ellison, according to the mail I looked at."

"You robbed his mail?" He was incredulous.

I plopped into one of his soft chairs, "No. I just looked at the addressee and put it back.

"Did anyone see you?" I had his attention.

"Just the butler. I ran before he could catch me." I replied. "Then I went by the offices of the union."

"My girl works there. You must have seen her."

That answered that question. "She's the receptionist, right?" He nodded in the affirmative. That answered one of my questions.

275

"Is she in tight with either of the bosses?" That was my second query.

He didn't hesitate, "No, it's just a job. Which one of the men did you meet?"

"Neither. They kept me waiting over a half hour before I walked out. Have you ever seen either of them?"

"No. I was only up there once, and I got distracted by Judy. Neither guy came out of the office while I was there. Do you have a picture of your guy, what do you call him, Joe?"

"That's right." I reached into my jacket and produced the photo, wrinkled by now. I handed it to him.

"Good looking guy, isn't he?"

"Yeah, I guess. I never thought about it. If I could get a look at one of those guys, either Ellison or Small, I'd at least be able to rule them out as Joe, because I understand they look a lot alike."

"That's what Judy tells me. She's never sure which one she's talking to, except for the voices. They're different."

"In what way?" I questioned.

"She didn't really say, and I didn't ask." Jerry replied. Then he added, "Can I help you with any of this?"

"You might be able to at that. I didn't want to get you involved, because it might be dangerous, if you ask the wrong people. My girl was already shot over this. But I need to find out who Joe is, and I'm at a standstill. I'm not sure where to go right now."

Jerry thought for a minute then said, "What if I go up to see Judy, just casual like, and go to use the bathroom, and go through the wrong door into the office. I might get a look at one or both of them that way."

"It might work at that. Just be careful."

"Don't worry." Jerry answered, "Everyone knows I'm kind of unconscious, and they won't think a thing about it."

"Okay, thanks. I'll check back with you tomorrow. I don't have to take Rachel to the airport until two, so I'll run by your place after that."

"You better make it five. I might have an unloading job tomorrow. I think a cargo ship is coming in."

"You've got it. I should go check on Rachel now. I haven't talked to her since early this morning. She might be sore."

"When do I get to meet this ravishing beauty of yours?"

"I'm afraid it will have to wait until the next time we're here, or if you come to San Diego. I'm worried about her showing her face in Chicago, at least until the guys who attacked her are put away."

We left it at that, and I headed for the hotel. There was no sign of the car that had been tailing me earlier.

I was pretty sure I'd be in trouble for having left my girl for so long, and I was right.

"Did you forget I was here? Or lose the phone number?"

"Sorry kid," I said as I kissed her on the cheek. I was aiming for her lips, but she turned away, pouting. "I got so busy, I just forgot. It won't happen again."

"You got that right." She replied. Then she turned back to me and gave me a proper kiss. I think I was forgiven.

We watched a Hopalong Cassidy movie before turning in. I was beat, but I managed to make love to my girl anyway.

Chapter Nineteen

Rachel was still sleeping when I dressed quietly and left the hotel room. I'd gotten an idea in the middle of the night while I was watching her chest move up and down in rhythm, and feeling like the luckiest guy in the world. She was even beautiful with her eyes closed.

I stopped at the desk on my way out to check the phone book. I found the address I was looking for and went to my rental car, which was in the hotel parking lot. I looked around to see if I would need to shake a tail, before heading to the local FBI office.

I found the place easily enough, and when I walked in, there were three men I assumed to be agents at three separate desks spread out throughout the small room. There was no counter. I just stood there until one of them, a dark-haired Latino-looking man in a blue suit, noticed me. He closed the folder he was apparently working on and walked up to me, looking me up and down as he did.

"May I help you sir?"

"I hope so." I answered, as I pulled out my wallet with my Private Investigator's license.

He took the wallet, and studied the license. "What do you need with the FBI Mister Dunn?"

I took the ID back and said, "It's a long story. Can we sit down somewhere?" He obliged by leading me back to his desk and pulling up another chair.

"Okay, what have you got?" He picked up a pen and was poised to write down what was said. "We need to make this official. My name is agent Fernandes just so you'll know who took the report, in case someone should ask."

I started at the beginning and laid out everything I did and saw, who I talked to, and who I didn't. He never said a word until I was done. "What do you think?"

"We are aware of some of what you've reported, how I'm not at liberty to say at this time. There's been no report of a missing person as far as I know, so that's rather strange. As far as the Chicago police are concerned, they're a pretty decent bunch, with a few exceptions as in any law enforcement agency. We'll have to keep an eye on that. You don't know the name of the officer who struck you?" He made it a question.

"No. He was a rather big guy, with a large waistline. He was Caucasian and balding. What little hair he did have was dark brown. He had a gruff voice. I saw him twice, as I mentioned in my report before. The officer with him didn't say much of anything. I had the feeling he didn't like what was happening."

"Well that should do it," he said putting down his pen. "How long are you going to be in town, Dunn, in case we need to get in touch with you."

"I hope to leave within a week. I'm getting married."

"Well, congratulations. Just a word of advice. You don't really have any official jurisdiction here, so you should let us handle the investigation from here on. I'd hate to see you hurt. These are dangerous people we're dealing with, and you don't want to break any more laws either."

"Right. What about that altercation I had?"

He thought for a second, and then answered, "We can't get involved in that. You're going to have to go back to court, even if you have to fly back to do it. I doubt that the judicial system will work fast enough to dispose of your case before you leave."

I thanked him for his time, shook hands and walked out into a surprisingly sunny day.

I figured to take Rachel to lunch before heading out to the airport. She didn't have to board until three.

The hotel lobby was reasonably quiet for late morning as I walked through to the elevator. Not so for my true love. She was fuming.

"Where have you been? I had hoped we could spend the day together, since it is apparently my last one here."

I reached for her but she pulled away. "No you don't you phony baloney," she said as she backed up. "You don't get off that easy.

You think you can just smooth things over any time you want by kissing me."

"No, I like to kiss you. It has nothing to do with anything else. You can be mad if you like, but as you say, we don't have much time, and I was hoping I could take you out to a nice place for lunch."

She softened some, and moved back toward me. "Lunch will probably make me like you again, but not much. Do I really have to go back?" Now she was selling me as she molded all of her five foot ten frame against me.

"We've been through this. It's too dangerous for you here. You have to go along with me on this. It won't be for long. I still want to marry you before the month is out."

"Well, all right, but I don't like it." She emphasized her words with a long kiss. "I'd much rather stay with you. Think what you'll be missing."

Now it was me who pulled away. I was getting too warm. "Grab your hat and coat. It's white out there, even though the sun is out, but it's hot enough to be summer in here."

She laughed. "At least I know I still have an effect on you. You were gone so long I was beginning to wonder."

Chapter Twenty

Carolyn Chase always considered herself a practical woman. Even as a child, she reasoned things out. She didn't just jump into something, even though it might seem to be a good idea at the time. She had few friends because they all seemed to be immature and childish compared to her.

Even when she first met Bob Chase, she was wary. He had to grow on her. When she finally realized that he was the man for her, still she went slowly. She'd seen other women who threw themselves at a man, only to be scarred and hurt almost beyond repair.

She was proud of her man, and her choice to become his bride. He had a good job, and a livable income. He was attractive in a manly way. He was educated, but didn't advertise it.

Carolyn had concerns about his transfer to Chicago, and they were only somewhat relieved when he called shortly after he had arrived there. He had said that he might not be able to check in with her as often as he'd like, but she shouldn't worry. She could call his boss, a man named Harry Shields, and he in turn would keep her up to date on what was going on, at least within reason.

The last time Bob called, he sounded stressed, which wasn't like the man she knew. She didn't want to add to his worries, so she kept the fact that she had had some vaginal bleeding to herself. Instead, she dutifully asked if he was eating regularly, and sleeping enough at night. He assured her he was. He had a habit of making a kissing sound with his lips before hanging up. That didn't happen the last time they spoke.

Their baby's birthday would have been on the day 1952 was ushered in, except that Carolyn had been rushed to the Olympic Memorial hospital on New Year's Eve with severe stomach cramps. The child was stillborn shortly after midnight.

There was no way to notify the would-be father. Carolyn was destitute and depressed, blaming everyone including and especially her husband for not being there for her.

It was February before she finally contacted Harry Shields in Chicago. The FBI chief couldn't tell her anything that would relieve her anxiety, just that he was on assignment, and would eventually check back in.

That was not acceptable to Carolyn Chase. She put an ad in the local newspaper advertising their home for rent, and when a nice family of three moved in, she flew to Chicago.

Harry Shields, usually unflappable, was shocked to find Carolyn Chase sitting in his outer office waiting to see him. He didn't know what to tell her. To say that his agent was missing and not heard from for nearly two months didn't seem to be an option for him, since the woman sitting across from him was obviously distraught already. He knew of her loss.

One of the stipulations Robert Chase had insisted upon, before he agreed to go undercover, was that the FBI monitor his wife's condition regularly, and provide any help that might be needed.

Shields had lived up to that responsibility, though Carolyn never knew it. He had engaged a doctor, at his own expense, to be on hand in case of complications during the birth. As it was, no one could have saved the child. His shared umbilical cord had wrapped around his neck, and choked off his food supply days before the delivery.

In this instance Shields could only reassure her that everything was being done to bring her husband back to her. He had in fact sent another field agent into the area incognito to ferret out the circumstances of Robert's disappearance. Nothing had turned up yet.

Carolyn was advised to go back to the Pacific Northwest to wait for word, which should be forthcoming soon. She didn't argue with the man, but neither did she return home. She found a reasonable hotel room downtown, and waited to hear about her loved one's whereabouts.

Chapter Twenty-one

Joe had not heard anything from Ivan or Rachel in a few days, and he was getting cabin fever. He'd been told not to venture out of his apartment, but he grew tired of reading magazines after the first day. He was no closer to finding out who he was than when he woke up in the park by the lake in Chicago.

The second day of his forced incarceration he wandered out into the daylight and found a movie theater. He watched a double-feature then had dinner at a small café. It was dark when he returned to his rooms.

He considered going to Chicago to force an end to his predicament, but quickly discarded the idea, realizing he had little money, only what Ivan had left him. Not only that but the fact that he didn't know who wanted him dead, or why, would give him no starting point even if he did make it to the large metropolis.

That night in his restlessness, while he tossed and turned, he remembered something. It might have been in a dream, he couldn't tell. He sat up, excited. Maybe his memory was returning.

It wasn't really an important fact, and didn't reveal to him who he was, but it was a start. He had seen the house in which he might have lived. It was a big place, with white pillars, as in the deep south. Maybe he came from a place like Alabama, or Louisiana. But he didn't have a southern drawl. He could have moved there from somewhere else though. It was too bad he couldn't see the house's surroundings, or the inside. That might have helped.

How had he gotten to Chicago? And Why? There were still so many questions, and only the one hint of an answer. Maybe another piece of the puzzle would be revealed to him soon. At least he now knew more than when he had retired for the night.

He was too excited to go back to sleep. There was no one he could call to share his news. He rose and went into the small apartment kitchen where he made a pot of coffee. He had decided to return to the hospital where Rachel had been to try to see the psychiatrist from before. Maybe they could unravel more of his past together. Dawn could not come soon enough.

After daybreak, and a quick breakfast, Joe took a bus from North Park to Pacific Beach where the hospital was located. He was still a little early for a psychiatrist's hours, so he went into the building's coffee shop to read the morning paper and kill time.

An article in the local section of the San Diego Union caught his eye. It seemed important somehow.

Fire destroys local union hall

At four this morning a passerby noticed smoke coming from the roof of the large building on the wharf off Harbor Drive. By the time fire engines arrived on the scene, the building was fully engulfed. The flames were extinguished by daybreak, but crews remain at the premises to check for spot fires. No reason for the fire had been determined at this writing.

It was the same address that Joe had found on the piece of paper in his pants the day he awoke soaking wet on the lawn of the Chicago park.

He forgot about seeing the psychiatrist. He had to find a way to return to the Midwest. Then it occurred to him that anybody could panhandle. He would need around one hundred dollars to get him to Chicago by bus, and for expenses while he was there. He would worry about the rest of it later.

He made a new sign. It couldn't be too elaborate lest he give away the fact he was no longer destitute, at least not for now. He found an old piece of cardboard. It was creased in the middle, having been folded. There was a food stain that would be visible to the casual reader. Joe knew that only maybe one in five travelers would look at the sign, but if he found a busy corner, where there was a stop light, enough would see it. They might feel guilty for their good fortune after seeing him in ragged, dirty clothes.

The words on his cardboard were less important than his appearance, because few would read all of it. He wrote VET in large letters, then a few other words to invoke pity. His mind wandered and he wondered if he really had been in the war? After visiting a thrift store he was ready.

His devious plan worked to perfection, and after only two days he was ready to venture east with nearly one hundred dollars in his now immaculate trousers, after the purchase of a one-way bus ticket to Chicago. Had he spent one more day on the San Diego sidewalk he might have had enough to purchase a plane ticket. As it was, his last day outside had turned colder with a brisk sea-breeze under a blanket of grey clouds sweeping in from the nearby ocean.

Chapter Twenty-two

The wind was howling and whipping around as we stepped out onto the street from the hotel. Rachel had checked out of her room, but I kept mine. We took a cab to the airport so I didn't have to bother parking. A porter was right there to retrieve her bags, and we walked unencumbered into the huge terminal at O'hare.

Thanks to the porter we were able to bypass the ticket counter and head right out to the concourse. When they called the flight we embraced, and I felt a temptation to tell her to cancel out and stay with me, but I resisted, and I watched as she disappeared onto the stairs leading to the tarmac. When she reappeared heading out to the waiting plane I heard my name on the building's loudspeaker. I turned away, looking for someone to advise me where to go for a phone call. When I finally picked up the courtesy phone, the line was dead. Whoever had needed to reach me must have given up when it took so long for me to answer. I reasoned that it couldn't be that important, although I was curious who would be that impatient to just hang up.

I decided to swing by Jerry's place to see if he had discovered who occupied the office at the union, but first I had to hail a cab to take me back to my hotel parking lot to retrieve my car. It was nearly five by the time I reached my friend's house.

I knocked on his door and waited. No answer. I rang the bell. Same result. He had known I was coming by after I took Rachel to the airport, so I doubted he was sleeping. I walked around to the only side of the house with a walkway. On the back porch I peered inside the dark building. I couldn't see anything. Maybe he had to work late, I reasoned, as I went back to my car.

I thought I might have a message when I reached the hotel, but no such luck. The clerk behind the desk double-checked for me, just in case it had been overlooked.

I decided to drive back to Jerry's house and wait for him. The lights were still off when I arrived and walked onto his porch. Just to be safe I knocked loudly before going back to my car, which was parked right out front.

More than an hour passed and still no Jerry. I was beginning to worry that something had happened to him. He didn't have a garage, and his car was nowhere to be seen on the street in front or near his house. There was plenty of room to park, so it wasn't as if he had to find a place around the corner.

After another half hour I drove to the FBI office. I didn't trust the police, and I wanted to have someone of authority check the inside of my friend's house. Maybe he had fallen or something.

Shields wasn't there, but the agent on duty in the office told me he would relay the message by phone and Shields would probably call me soon. I drove back to Jerry's and waited outside.

By eight o'clock I decided to take matters into my own hands. I went around back, found a window that looked as if it might lead to the bedroom, and broke it. I looked around to see if anyone noticed. When I saw or heard nothing I carefully climbed through into what was indeed a bedroom. After closing the curtain I fumbled along the wall for a light switch. I found it on the second wall I tried.

The bed had been slept in, but I reasoned that it could have been used the night before, Jerry being a bachelor and probably untidy like most of us.

I found him in the front room. He was wearing work clothes. He was only a few feet from the door. He was tied to a chair, and had obviously been beaten before the killer took his life. There was a pool of blood on the floor that was congealed. His throat had been cut. It probably happened before I came to his place earlier.

I felt sick. I had seen dead bodies before but this wasn't the same. He was my friend. He had saved my life. He was a marine. He deserved to grow old with his loved ones around him when he passed.

There was no doubt in my mind that August Schell was responsible. It was his style. He hadn't killed me because I had information he wanted. I knew where Joe was, and until he found out I would remain alive. What August Schell and Chris Ellison, or Aaron Small didn't know was that now I was going to come after them. I knew Ellison worked out of the Longshoreman's union office, and he lived in the big house out by the park at the lake. I would find him, and I would bet that Schell wouldn't be far away.

I placed a call, this time to the police. I did it anonymously. I was in enough hot water with them and I couldn't afford to be picked up, not yet.

I left by the same window from which I had gained access to the house. I hadn't touched the body, though I wanted to cut him loose. Eventually they would probably track my fingerprints, but by then I hoped I would have finished my business in Chicago. The only thing on my mind at that point was revenge.

I stopped by a gun shop on my way back to the hotel, and purchased a used .38 revolver. I also picked up a knife. I didn't care if Schell was alive or dead when I slit his throat from ear to ear.

Chapter Twenty-three

The bus from San Diego was crowded, and Joe got the last seat. He was near the back, which was fine with him. He could people watch from that vantage point. It would help him pass the time. As it was he would have to change busses in L.A., and the ride to Chicago would take nearly three days.

He'd had no further flashes into his past since the one, and there was no guarantee there would be others. This might be a total wild goose chase, but it was better than dying of boredom in his apartment.

All he had to go on was that his amnesia was somehow tied to Longshoremen. As far as he knew he'd never been on the docks, either in San Diego or Chicago. His options had been limited by the fire at the wharf. It was too bad he didn't think of checking there before the blaze.

He had nearly an hour's wait at Union Station in Los Angeles-not enough time to venture outside for sightseeing, so he bought a San Diego Evening Tribune and settled into a less than comfortable wooden seat.

He was hoping there would be a follow-up article about the fire, and on the front page of the local section he found it.

Arson strongly suspected at Longshoremen's Union.

Investigators from the Fire department found evidence of an incendiary device in a bathroom of the building.

No suspects have been identified at this time. No bodies were found at the scene, and there were no witnesses. Police are still investigating.

The article went on to provide background information about the building, and its purpose. There were interviews with the principals involved with the day to day operation of the company, along with comments from high-ranking fire department officers.

The bus leaving L.A. was on time. Joe found himself sitting on the aisle. Next to him was a rather homely middle-aged woman. Across the passageway a pretty young Mexican-looking woman wrestled with two children crowded together, trying to get them settled.

It seems as if there is always one or two unruly passengers on a bus or streetcar filled with people. Maybe even a train. On this trip it was a couple of young men seated directly behind the lady with the kids. They had obviously brought a bottle aboard, and they were guzzling the foul smelling stuff.

Joe could sense there would be trouble with the two, and he didn't have long to wait. By the time the bus left San Bernardino, they were loud and boisterous. Everyone in the back half of the bus was becoming very uncomfortable.

Soon the one who was sitting right behind the Mexican lady reached over and put his bottle right in front of her nose. "Hey good-looking, you want some of this?"

She tried to pull back from the liquor but there was no room. "No thank you."

"Aw come on, it will be good for you, loosen you up."

At this point she was squirming, trying to distance herself. "I said No!"

The driver was too far away and was oblivious to what was happening in the rear of his bus. The woman's children were becoming frightened.

Joe didn't want to get involved, but he remembered when Rachel was shot and he had done nothing. This time silence didn't seem to be an option. "Why don't you leave the lady alone? She said she didn't want any."

"Who the hell are you asshole? You'd better stay out of this."

"I'm already in it man. Pull the bottle back now!"

The man in the other seat, who'd also been drinking, stood up. "Who the hell do you think you are? I'm gonna kick your butt."

Before he could take a step Joe rose and, seemingly in one motion, with his hand flat, hit his adversary in his neck. The other man's hands went to his throat. He couldn't breathe. Joe kicked his legs out from under him with his left leg, and the assailant fell on his back in the passageway. He was still gagging. Joe reached for the other man, but he raised his arms in surrender, his bottle still clutched in his right hand.

Meanwhile the man on the floor of the bus was beginning to breathe normally again, and the driver, now becoming aware of the commotion, stopped the big rig on the side of the road. By the time he came back to intervene, the fighting was over.

The lady sitting next to Joe said, "It was those two," pointing at the drunks. Their smelly breaths made it obvious who she was talking about.

The driver raised his voice, "Okay you two, off the bus right now!"

The one who Joe had hit was the first one out the door, followed quietly by his friend. Their party was over.

At the first scheduled stop for the bus, Joe found a table by himself, and was attacking a roast beef sandwich when he heard a woman speaking.

"May we sit down?" Joe looked up from his meal to see the woman and her children who had sat across the aisle from him. She had a pleasant voice with no hint of a Spanish accent. The kids were staring at him with an awestruck look on their small faces.

"Sure, step into my office." He said. It was his first attempt at humor since he couldn't remember when.

They were at the truck stop where the bus had pulled over for a forty-five minute lunch break. The place was just west of Barstow, California.

297

As the three of them crowded into the booth across from Joe's side of the table, she spoke, "My name is Ariel." It sounded like AHriel. The way she pronounced it just seemed to roll off her tongue.

"That's a very pretty name, and unusual. I'm not sure I've heard it before." He didn't add that he didn't remember hearing any names at all except Ivan and Rachel. It wasn't her problem.

She was speaking again, "I wanted to thank you for what you did back there." Joe started to answer, but she interrupted, "I was not afraid for myself, but for the children. They have not seen violence before. I'm glad that the first time was for good, not evil."

That was a strange way to put it, he thought. This was an interesting woman. She really was not much more than a teen-aged girl, he guessed she was about twenty-two. She was pretty too. He hadn't really paid much attention before. Her jet black hair glistened in the light from the restaurant. Her eyes were probably brown, but they looked nearly black. She was slender, maybe one hundred and twenty pounds, which was just about right for her height, which he guessed to be around five-five.

"My children are named Juan, he's five, and my four-year old is Jessica." Joe had a questioning look on his face, as she answered his obvious next query, "I wanted to give both my children American names, but I could not convince my husband, who is Spanish, until our second child."

298

"Where is your husband now?" It was the logical next question.

"We are divorced. He returned to Spain." and she added "I think."

"I see."

"We are travelling to Chicago. I have a job waiting, and an apartment for the three of us."

After their lunch, Juan and Jessica moved into the now vacated seats behind where they were before, and Joe moved into the seat next to Ariel. She was pleasant to talk to. He had been cooped up for so long that he yearned for some adult conversation.

As the distance from where they had started increased, and the temperature followed suit with their penetration into the desert, the four of them seemed to belong together. In Kingman, Arizona Joe watched Juan and Jessica while Ariel used the facilities. With the stop in Flagstaff for dinner they once again all sat together. Left unsaid was how Joe had been able to react so strongly to the danger posed by the two drunks on the bus, though he found himself wondering why he had acted the way he did, so forcefully. Where did he learn such things? And why was it so easy to talk to this stranger he shared his meals with?

"A penny for your thoughts." Ariel's father had used that term while she was growing up in East Los Angeles, long before she had moved south to San Diego. Joe had seemed to be far away. He hadn't touched his food.

299

"I was just thinking that it's easy talking to you. You have a knack for putting people at ease, at least you do with me."

She laughed softly, "I'm a very talented person. I should pat myself on the back."

"No, really. I find myself wanting to tell you all my secrets, if I had any."

"Do you?" She looked into his blue eyes, thinking, 'I don't know anything about this strange man with violence in him, and yet I feel completely safe with him.' "Who are you Joe? Is that really your name?" Before he could answer she continued, " And where did you come from, I don't mean now, but in the beginning?"

When she paused for a breath he answered. "I don't know the answer to your questions. I'm pretty sure my name isn't Joe. That was given to me by a fellow named Ivan Dunn. He picked me up on the street in San Diego when I was desperate. I had lost my memory. I don't remember anything that happened before that day in January. I could have a family, kids. I just don't know."

Instinctively, Ariel reached across the table and took his hand in hers. Her children giggled. She put her index finger to her lips signaling for them to be silent.

"How will you find out, Joe? That name does seem to fit you. I can see you being a Joe. It's a strong name, and you certainly are, but it's gentle in a way too. It implies that you are trustworthy, and honest."

"How do you know all this?"

"Intuition and experience," She giggled, "I'm very old you know."

"You can't be more than twenty-two now."

"Thanks for that. You're right, but don't you tell anybody. My experience argument will fly out the window." The twinkle that appeared in her eyes went well with her broad smile.

"So what happened with your marriage Ariel?"

"Please don't judge me for what I'm about to tell you. I was but sixteen when I found out I was with child. Tomas was eighteen and a senior in high school. He seemed dashing to me, like the heroes in books. He had come from Spain with his parents in 1940 to escape the fascists. He wasn't like the Mexicans I had grown up with. He seemed worldly, and the boys in my neighborhood were just children still. I was only a child myself, and very impressionable. Tomas's parents were strongly against our marriage, but consented, to legitimize our baby."

At this point in her story Ariel glanced at Juan, fearful he might hear. The boy was busy teasing his sister, and was oblivious to what his mother was saying.

"I had to leave school, and by the time Jessica was born, Tomas and I had grown apart. We were becoming different people. I was the practical one by that time, and he didn't want the responsibility of a family. My husband left me, and went back to Spain, presumably to fight for his country. I moved in with my parents, went back to school to get my diploma, leaving them to babysit. I received a scholarship to a small teaching college, obtained a divorce from my absent spouse and, after a time as a student teacher, graduated to the real thing. I'm on my way to Chicago to take a job at a high school there. Now you know everything about me."

Ariel looked around the café, and seeing no passengers said, "We had better get back to our ride before they leave us here."

By the time the bus left Gallup, New Mexico the two of them were holding hands like dating teenagers.

Chapter Twenty-five

I wasn't sure what my next move would be, but I knew I had to find the one-eared one, and settle things for Jerry. I headed back to my hotel to change clothes, and formulate a plan. I had suddenly become the hunter, and Joe's identity no longer filled my thoughts. I was glad that Rachel was out of harm's way. The scum I was dealing with had not hesitated to shoot her, when she posed no threat to them.

As I passed through the hotel lobby, I was stopped by the desk clerk. "I have a message for you Mr. Dunn." He handed me an envelope. When I was in the elevator I glanced at it. It was slightly wrinkled, as if it had been in someone's pocket. My name was printed on it in bold letters.

Once in my room I opened the envelope. There was a single sheet of white paper inside. My hand began to shake as I read the words. 'WE HAVE YOUR GIRL. YOU KNOW WHERE TO FIND HER!'

That didn't make sense. I saw Rachel board the plane for San Diego. No I didn't! I had to answer the phone at the airport. But how could they pull it off? She was only a few steps from safety when I turned away. Maybe they were bluffing. They were desperate to question me, just before they ended my life.

She had to be at the house by the lake park. They knew I'd been there. If I went in with gun blazing I could hit Rachel. Going up to the front door without my weapon drawn would be a death sentence for me, and wouldn't help her. These people had shown they were capable of the most destructive violence , and wouldn't understand anything but force. I had no options as far as I could tell, but I had to find a way to get her out of there unharmed. I was the one who had gotten her into this. If I hadn't picked up Joe out on the street, if I had just kept going, and lived with the guilt the panhandlers counted on to keep them in booze or whatever, Rachel would be safe now, and we would likely have been married and living happily ever after. Now all the money I had would not secure protection for my girl or me.

Then a thought occurred to me. I could alert the FBI to the kidnapping and enlist their assistance. I had met Harry Shields, and he seemed like a decent sort. At least I might not be in this alone. I would need all the help I could come up with.

I was in luck when I walked into the FBI office. Shields was there. When he saw me he motioned me into his office. Once seated I told him the story, beginning with Rachel's abduction at O'hare International. I related what I had found at Jerry Greenway's house. He told me he had heard it on the police scanner about my friend.

"Were you the one who called it in?" He asked, with a frown on his face.

"Yeah. I broke into his house when I couldn't raise him by phone or at the door. I didn't touch the body though."

"The police are going to love you when they find out you were in there."

"I know, but it can't get much worse, can it?"

"We'll see. I should just turn you in to them now, in the spirit of cooperation, you know?" Now he had a slight grin on his otherwise somber countenance.
"But you and I both know they'd fry you for it, and given the fact of police corruption in this city, I think I'll hold off for now."

"Thanks for that. Have you heard anything from the agent on the inside?" I remembered him saying that there was someone who had infiltrated the gang.

"No. But that's not too unusual. He might put himself in danger by contacting us. Your girl getting picked up has changed everything. We were just going to wait it out until our guy had the goods on that mob. Now I don't think we have that luxury."

"That's good for me. I need the help getting Rachel clear of them."

"Hold on. You're involved enough as it is. I can't let a civilian get hurt on my watch if I can help it."

"With all respect, you can't stop me. I've got nothing to lose with the law after me anyway. And my life is in there."

"Well I can't legally tie you down, but I can hold you for the Chicago police," and he added, "if I'm so inclined."

I saw my opening, and told him my plan. It had just come to me on the way over to the FBI office.

"It might work at that, but the Federal Government can't spend the kind of money it will take to pull it off."

"This one's on me," I said. "I've just got the cash lying around anyway."

"It's nice dealing with people with deep pockets." He observed.

As the miles went by and Chicago drew closer, Joe and Ariel became more familiar with one another. As that happened the amnesiac began feeling something like deja vu. He had the strange feeling he had done this before.

Ariel related how, growing up in East Los Angeles, she had learned to speak Spanish and English simultaneously. She became comfortable with both languages, but her thoughts were in English. She preferred the more complicated tongue, perhaps because most of the children around her spoke it.

By the time the Greyhound bus reached Joplin, Missouri along Route 66, more of Joe's memory had returned. He remembered a girl, a woman really, a pretty one. They had been close. He knew that much but he couldn't remember her name. Something had happened. She had left him or was just gone from his life. He couldn't remember.

"Joe, you were off somewhere again. Where were you?" Ariel jolted him back to the present.

306

"I'm sorry. I just remembered something else, but I'm not sure what it means."

"What is it?" She asked.

Joe was so comfortable talking and being with Ariel, that he didn't want to keep anything from her. "I remembered another woman."

"What was her name?"

"I can't remember."

"Do you know where she is now?"

"No. Not only that, I don't even know if we still cared for one another when I lost my memory. I can just see her in my mind."

Ariel looked sad. "We just met, but I don't want you to be involved with someone else. Does that sound selfish?"

"I don't think so. I'm flattered that you would say it. I want to give this thing with us a chance, whatever it is."

"I do too. I'll be honest though, I'm concerned about the anger you showed on the bus earlier, and the violence. You seem like a gentle man, and I like that, but the other is there somewhere too. And that worries me. I have the children to consider."

"That's reasonable. I don't know where it came from either. If and when I find out, you'll be the first one I come to."

"I believe you." She took his hand, and kissed him on the forehead.

"You missed," he said, "My lips are down a little lower "

"You really are a rake, aren't you?" And then, not waiting for a reply she added, "I'm glad we found each other."

Chapter Twenty-six

For my plan to work I'd need a fire truck, and a few uniforms. I figured the FBI would supply the bodies   to fill the firemen's uniforms.

I found a junk yard not far from town. They had an old model fire truck, but it would need a little work. I hired a mechanic, and took him to my relic. After checking out the engine, he assured me he could get it running that afternoon. So far so good. I called Shields to see if he had had any luck securing the uniform disguises. He told me he was able to get five. That would have to do it.

Under my plan I would be able to keep my gun. I wasn't going through the front door. Success would depend on finding Rachel, hopefully before I was detected.

Down at the dock I was able to rent a small boat and motor. If I approached the house from the water, I figured there would be less chance of being detected. I would have to find a way in from the back of the house while the ersatz fire department created the diversion of spraying the perfectly good house with the fire hoses from the fake fire truck.

Shields was also working on obtaining floorplans for the big house. It was possible we might be able to determine what area they could be holding Rachel in. That was a long shot, but so was my idea for gaining entrance to the place and maintaining complete surprise.

I had no choice really. If my girl was to survive this mess, we'd probably have to kill or incapacitate everyone in the place. Our best card was surprise.

Rachel was a civilian. She didn't deserve any of this. I cursed myself over and over for the way it had happened. Being a good Samaritan sucked. If I had just stepped on the gas, or given him a buck, instead of picking him up and listening to his story-if August Schell hadn't put a bullet in Rachel's side, or I hadn't gone to Chicago in the first place-if Jerry Greenway had kept his mouth shut, and not told his girlfriend about my having Joe-if,if,if. Rachel and I would be married, and Jerry would still be alive to have his heart broken by his Mata Hari, two-faced woman.

So now I'd go in there, guns blazing, hoping to kill them before they got me. The odds weren't good, but there was no other way that I could see.

At three o'clock that fateful day I stopped back by the FBI office to take a look at the house's floor plan. We synchronized our watches for seven-thirty that night. We couldn't afford to wait another day. It would take me about an hour to navigate Lake Michigan to the park area, so I planned to shove off from the pier at six just to make sure I arrived on time. I bought some dark clothes, along with a black stocking cap to minimize the chances of being seen, either outside the house or when I searched for Rachel before confronting the mob guys.

At precisely five-thirty I walked out of the hotel, retrieved my rental car, and drove toward the pier. Then everything unraveled.

I saw the flashing red lights about a block from the dock where my boat was waiting. 'Maybe they're not after me' I hoped. I pulled over, and looked at my watch instinctively. Time was critical. I even crossed my fingers, but it didn't help.

In my side-view mirror I saw the big cop who had emphasized his point of view with his nightstick coming toward the driver's side door. His partner, the silent one, had exited the passenger side of their patrol car, and taken a place just behind my right rear fender. His hand was on his holster.

"Step out of the car please." At this point he was being polite. That changed quickly as soon as I was clear of the door. "Face the car and spread 'em", he growled.

I could do nothing but comply. When he patted me down he quickly found my piece, and removed it. He didn't check further, so I was able to retain my knife. I still felt naked.

He pushed me into the back seat of the cop car, not bothering to assure that I didn't hit my head while entering. It didn't hurt much.

I hoped I would have a chance to talk my way out of the police station when I would be around more reasonable officers than the nightstick guy, who obviously had it in for me.

311

I would do my protesting where it might do more good.

Those hopes were dashed when I realized we were heading north away from town. "Where are we going, on a picnic?"

"Shut up wise guy."

As we headed out Lakeshore Drive, I guessed where they were taking me. The driver's partner finally spoke, "Are you sure about this? We should just take him in, and charge him with possession of a firearm."

The big guy would have none of this. "Naw. Ellison will pay big for us to deliver him there."

So I was going to my destination anyway. I would be going through the front door, and without my gun, but you can't have everything. At least I would finally get a look at Ellison. If I could stall them from killing me until seven-thirty, I still might have a chance to save Rachel, but I wouldn't bet on it.

Chapter Twenty-seven

By the time Joe's bus pulled into the service bay in downtown Chicago all his memory had returned. He didn't know who sapped him, it was from behind, but he knew his own name, and why it happened. He wasn't sure why he survived the attempt on his life. Historically bodies were weighted down and didn't surface. It was one thing he didn't understand. Maybe he would never know.

He said goodbye to Ariel and the kids, with a heavy heart. He felt he would not see them again, since he might not survive the confrontation that was to come.

He needed a gun for what he was planning to do. He didn't want one that was traceable, so after renting a car, he visited a firearms shop he had done illegal business with before. The Thompson sub-machine gun he bought with money left over from his street work would do the trick, he thought.

It was already dark when Joe reached the house by the park. He had stashed his car a few blocks away, and walked through the grassy park to behind the big place, his Tommy gun hidden under his overcoat. There was a door leading into the basement that he knew he could jimmy. No one was expecting him so the cellar most likely wouldn't be guarded.

***

At nearly the same time the police car stopped a few blocks away to the north of the house. I was unaware that Joe was even in the city. The three of us made our way on foot, with me being forced to lead, the two uniformed cops a few steps behind.

A man with gun drawn let us in. It was the same one who had driven Chris Ellison to the union hall, the man who had chased me down the street after seeing me raid the Ellison mailbox. Now he was dressed in a more normal manner, in a dark suit with a hat. In those days it was a transitional period, with some men wearing fedoras or wide-brimmed hats, others wearing caps, and some remaining bare-headed. In most cases it depended on how much hair remained on an individual's head.

The gunman waved us inside. It appeared that we were on the main floor. There would be an upstairs where the bedrooms were located, and a basement that actually would be at ground level, adjacent to the park, since we had walked up a flight of stairs to reach the porch leading to the main entrance. From the plans I had seen, the living spaces-kitchen, dining room, and living room, along with two bathrooms, were on that middle or main floor. It would be likely that Rachel was being held upstairs in one of the bedrooms, that is if she was still alive. I felt a chill just thinking of the possibility she may not have survived.

Once inside the spacious living room I saw four men in addition to my two escorts- the one-eared August Schell, that guy Manny from the union hall, and two others I had never seen before. The tall one had to be Chris Ellison. At first I was a little relieved to see that Manny was mixed up in all this. It justified my threatening him, at least in my mind. But then I was boiling when I thought he might have had a hand in my friend's death. I really wanted a chance to even the score. However, under the present circumstances, It didn't appear that I would get it.

The stranger I assumed to be Ellison said, rather calmly, "Keep your eye on him Benny. One false move you drill him."

August Schell smiled. He knew that was usually his job, but Benny was being tested.

"Did you kill Jerry Greenway?" I spit it out, looking directly at Schell.

"Yeah." Was his answer, "and I enjoyed it, too."

"That's enough of that!" snapped the one who was obviously in charge.

I looked at him, really for the first time. I did a double take. He looked just like Joe. His voice was similar, but more husky, as if he had a cold.

"Look Mister Ellison," it was the one called Benny speaking now, "Why don't we bring the girl down, and use her to force him to tell us what we want to know?"

So I was right about mister lookalike. I glanced at my watch. Sixteen minutes until

315

cavalry time. I had to stretch this out. "Sure I'll tell you everything you need. Why don't you just put your guns away? We'll all sit down and have a quiet chat, then go our own way, no hard feelings." Fifteen minutes.

"Why don't you just tell us now?" It was Schell speaking, a little agitated.

I knew they wouldn't dispose of me before they learned where Joe was, so I pushed it a little. "What was that, one-ear?"

I pushed the right button. He turned red, and rushed me. I managed to pull my six-inch switchblade knife from my sock just in time. As I fumbled for the button, I could almost feel his breath on my face. Click. He looked down but too late as I came up with a thrust into his midsection. I was aiming for just below the sternum, so I was close. He doubled over. I stepped around him, and then wrapping my left arm around his chest, I pulled him back to me. With my right hand I scraped the knife blade across his throat from left back to right, plunging it deeper into the soft tissue as I went. I must have got the carotid artery, because blood gushed from his neck, and his hands went instinctively to his throat. It was only seconds before he went limp in my arms. I let him fall lifelessly to the carpet, his warm blood splattered on my arm.

As I looked at his still body, there was no trace of the young Austrian boy who had become a legend to the French people he defended. No honor in death, just a ragged piece of flesh that had gone the way of so many that he himself had dispatched to the hell reserved for killers.

Both the hood named Benny and Manny pointed their guns at me, but before they could pull the trigger, the one called Ellison yelled "Stop!", and they did. It was a good thing. I was sure my now bloody knife would not match up well with a bullet. Twelve minutes.

"Why don't you just tell us where he is, and end all this?" There was no remorse in his voice for his fallen comrade.

"Look Ellison, if that's your name, I don't know what you're talking about."

"It's a little late to play dumb isn't it? We know he was at your house."

"Then just go pick him up, whoever he is."

"Listen, smart ass, we know he's not there now. If you want to leave here alive, you'll tell us what we want to know."

"Yeah, and I'll just bet you'll let me go." Five minutes, more or less. I couldn't look at my watch without drawing Ellison's attention to it. There was no clock in the room that I could see. "Besides, I won't tell you anything until I see Rachel, and know that you haven't harmed her."

"She's all right. So you do know where the man you call Joe is. What is he to you? You don't even know his real name."

"Why don't you tell me?" I could hear a faint siren off in the distance.

"I'm losing my patience Dunn." He looked in Benny's direction. "Go get the girl.

We're going to end this now, one way or the other."

I was hoping for the other, as the siren, which had become louder, stopped. In less than a minute, and before Benny reached the stairs leading up to where Rachel was, the windows were being splashed with water.

"What the hell?" Ellison yelled. "Manny go see what's going on."

As Manny opened the front door, a man dressed in a fireman's uniform pushed his way in, his gun drawn.

At the same time a door leading to the basement opened, and there stood Joe, a machine gun in his right arm, his left hand on the trigger.

I don't know who fired first, but with the first shot I dove behind a davenport, away from the line of fire. The rat tat tat tat that followed sounded like a hundred guns had fired at the same time. A body fell next to me. It was the nightstick cop. I pulled his gun from its holster. His hand was on it, but it hadn't even cleared. I heard someone yell FBI, but the gunfire continued. When it stopped, I took a chance and looked out from behind the couch. There were only three men left standing.

Joe hadn't moved from his place by the basement door. He was looking around to see if anyone was still a threat.

Benny was flashing an FBI shield, his gun aimed at Joe. Joe put his weapon down, and raised his arms, in surrender.

The other survivor was the FBI man in fireman gear, who apparently was wearing body armor.

I rushed upstairs. I found Rachel in the first bedroom I searched. She was tied to a chair, a gag in her mouth. She was alive!

I quickly removed the gag, and then attacked the ropes that bound her, as she exclaimed, "Oh Ivan, am I glad to see you!"

"I'm sorry I didn't get here sooner baby. Are you okay?"

"I am now," she said, as she wrapped her arms around me, and gave me a kiss that lasted at least a minute. "I could hear gunfire below me. What happened?"

"I'm not sure I know, but Joe's here, and he saved the day, along with the FBI." I was being honest. I had no idea what had gone on while I was behind that couch. Obviously Joe had regained his memory. I didn't know how he fit into the whole thing. But I was going to find out.

Chapter Twenty-eight

When Rachel and I stepped off the stairs onto the main floor of the big old house, we were greeted by Harry Shields.

"It was a pretty good operation, I think. None of my men were shot, and you survived with your girl. We have Ellison in custody, and I got my undercover man back unharmed.

"Wait a minute," I muttered, "I thought Ellison was dead. I saw him on the floor. He wasn't moving."

"Naw, that was Aaron Small you saw. He had assumed Ellison's identity when he went missing."

"I'm confused. Do you mean to tell me the guy I know as Joe is really Chris Ellison?"

"That's right. Small tried to kill Ellison, and he assumed his identity when he thought the murder had been carried out."

"I thought he looked like Joe, rather Ellison, when I got a good look at him."

"Yeah, he shaved off his moustache, and dyed his hair a darker shade. He fooled everyone."

"Why did he do that?" I was still bewildered.

"I'll let our agent Robert Chase catch you up on that."

The man I knew as Benny stepped up. "It all started when Chris Ellison told Small he was leaving the organization, and laying out the entire operation for the FBI. I was there when it happened."

"Why would he do that?"

"I'll let Ellison tell you that part. We transported him to the Federal jail. You can see him there."

Shields broke in, "I forgot, Robert, your wife is in town. She's at the Star Hotel. I think she might be glad to see you."

"Thanks boss, I'm on my way. She probably doesn't know if I'm alive or dead. I'll be lucky to talk my way out of this one." With that he was out the door.

After the door closed behind Chase, Shields said, "I don't think she'll be mad. She seems to really love the guy."

I told Rachel I would drop her off at the hotel before I went to see Joe at the jail. It would take me a while to get used to calling him Chris.

She would have none of that. "No you won't. I'm not letting you out of my sight. Besides, I'm curious too. Is Joe really a gangster?"

"It looks that way. We'll see what he has to say before judging him. He seemed like a decent sort before. But I can't get the thought out of my mind of him standing in that doorway with a Tommy gun. It was like an old poster from a thirties movie."

The Federal jail was a few miles south of downtown Chicago. They told us at the front desk they hadn't processed Chris Ellison yet, and it would be at least another hour before we could see him, if at all. The man at the desk informed us he would have to obtain permission from his superior before allowing us access to the prisoner.

Rachel and I used the time to go down the street to a café for coffee. We talked about what we would do in the weeks to come. The subject of marriage was front and center.

"I don't want to wait any longer, Rachel. I love you and I want to make an honest woman out of you."

"You won't get an argument from me. After what we've been through, marriage should be a breeze."

It was nearly nine o'clock when we returned to the jail. As luck would have it, Shields was there at the front desk. He obtained permission for us to see Joe.

They brought him out to the waiting room in handcuffs. The first thing he said was, "Rachel, I'm really glad you're all right."

"I think you had something to do with that Joe, and I'm grateful." I answered before Rachel had a chance.

She took his cuffed hands in hers, and smiling said, "Thank you Joe", and she squeezed his hands for emphasis.

"You two saved my life. You shouldn't be thanking me."

"Okay, we've got the pleasantries out of the way. Now what the hell happened?" I questioned with a frown on my face.

"I have to start back a few months before I met you. I was engaged to be married to a beautiful woman named Sally Singleton. She didn't like the life I was leading, and only

322

agreed to marry me if I went straight. To do that I would have to turn everything over to my partner Aaron Small. Aaron and I had known each other since we were kids. We weren't really friends but we had the same interests. Everyone thought we were brothers, we looked so much alike."

"I was willing to make a clean break, but Aaron didn't trust me. He was afraid I would eventually rat him out."

"Rat him out of what? What were you guys into?" I interrupted.

"It was protection. We sold it, and if the business owner wasn't buying, we managed to persuade him, one way or another."

"So what did the Longshoreman's union have to do with it?"

He continued, "I managed to become president of the Chicago local. We used the union to launder money from our extortion operation. We were going to expand to the west coast. That's why I had that San Diego address in my pocket."

"What happened? How did you end up in the lake, and how did you get out without drowning?"

"As I said, Aaron didn't trust me to keep my word. He went to see Sally to talk her into letting me stay connected. They had a big fight. He hit her, and in his rage he raped her. She was so ashamed that, when he left, she climbed into her bathtub-" he hesitated, and he was crying now, "and she slit her wrists."

Rachel reached out and hugged Joe, and held him close to her until his sobbing quieted.

"I found her, but I was too late. I went to find Aaron."

"How did you know he caused her to kill herself, or that someone else hadn't killed her, for that matter."

"She left a note, explaining everything."

"How do you know the note was authentic? Couldn't someone else have written it"

"No. It was in her handwriting, but that bastard Aaron might as well have done it. It happened because of him."

I said, "I didn't mean to interrupt, what happened then?"

"I found the son of a bitch. He was at my house by the lake. I beat the hell out of him, then told him I was going to the feds and lay out the whole operation for them. That would have got him twenty years. Then I blacked out. The next thing I remember is when I woke up soaking wet. You know the rest."

"When did your memory return?"

"I started getting bits and pieces the last few days in San Diego, then I pieced it all together on the bus coming here."

"You still haven't said how you survived the drowning attempt, or why Aaron Small was impersonating you?" I made it a question.

"I don't know the answer to the first part. I can only assume it was August Schell who sapped me. He and that guy Benny were

324

the only ones in the room at the time. As for Aaron taking over my identity, that's easy. Everything with the union was in my name. He could only control things if he was me. Otherwise he'd be out in the cold."

"So what happens next with you?"

"The FBI guy in charge said he was going to put in a good word for me. He thinks maybe I'll only get five years or so, because I helped out saving Rachel."

"Helped out hell, you were mostly responsible. I'll be forever grateful."

"I told you to knock that grateful stuff off. I brought all this down on you."

"Anyway, if there's anything we can do for you just let us know."

"You could get me some gum. My mouth is really dry from talking to you so much." He grinned.

I had to shake both his hands, considering his circumstances.

He said, "Send me a wedding invitation. You know I'd be there if I could."

Before leaving, Rachel kissed him on the cheek, and said, "You'll always be Joe to us. Look us up when you get out."

"I will, definitely, unless you change your mind in the meantime, and will be afraid to see me, remembering what happened the last time."

"It was just a walk in the park for us." I said it with a smile.

"As long as you're all right with everything, you could do me a huge favor on your way out of town?" It was said as a question.

"Sure. Name it."

"I met a really nice girl on the bus coming back here. I promised to keep in touch with her if I could. I think she needs to know why I won't be able to keep that promise."

"Give me her address, and I'll see to it."

He wrote out the numbers she had given him, along with her name.

"Ariel, that's a pretty name. We'll tell her about the man we knew as Joe, not Chris Ellison. I hope when you get released, that's who you'll be."

"Count on it."

Chapter Twenty-nine

I couldn't get reservations for Rachel and I to fly out until the next day, so after we got the best sleep either of us had since this whole thing with Joe started, I rose early. I still had some questions, such as how did Joe avoid drowning?

Rachel was still asleep when I dressed quietly and snuck out. The day seemed brighter, even though the sun was still on the horizon. Maybe it was my attitude. I had my girl back in one piece, and we would soon be back in what I considered God's country.

The FBI office was open, luckily. Harry Shields was nowhere to be seen, but the undercover guy, Robert Chase, was sitting at a desk attacking paperwork.

"Mr. Dunn I presume," he said as I walked up to his table.

"That's right. I want to tie up some loose ends in my mind, if you can spare the time."

"That would be a welcome pause for me. I've been at this report for nearly an hour. I hate this part of the job.".

"Did you find your wife? I remember hearing that she had come to Chicago to look for you."

"Yes, I did. She told me never to take an assignment like this one again, and I assured her there was no way I would."

"Good. I'm glad things worked out," and I added, "for all of us.

"That's for sure."

"There are a few loose ends I'd like to clear up. How did Chris Ellison survive the drowning attempt?"

"When he confronted Aaron Small, August Schell hit him from behind with a sap. He was out like a light. I was told to dump his body in the lake, making sure he didn't come up. That was lucky for him. I carried him downstairs into the basement, and tied his body to a cinder block, with Schell looking on. I was plenty worried about how to get out of that one. It's not something an FBI agent does. I put Ellison in a wheelbarrow that was stored there and took him out on the dock behind the house. Schell had gone back upstairs by then. Just before I dumped him in the drink, I untied the weight from his legs. I hoped that the cold water would wake him up in time, because I had to go through with it in case they were watching from above. As it turned out he woke up on his own, so I knew he'd be able to climb out by himself. It was about midnight, and no one was there to witness it."

"Okay, another thing. I dove behind the couch when the shooting started, and I don't know what really happened. Can you fill me in on that?"

"Well, I'll try. It all happened so fast, I'm not at all sure of my facts. I've been trying to get it down on paper, and maybe if I hash it out with you it'll become clearer in my head."

"Okay. When the FBI officers, dressed as firemen, arrived and began spraying the house with water, Joe, or Chris Ellison came into the room, apparently from a basement. Did he shoot first?"

"No. It was me. It looked like Manny was going to shoot you, and I couldn't let that happen."

"Smart choice. Thanks for that. And while I'm thinking of it, who kidnapped Rachel from the airport? She was almost to the plane the last time I saw her."

"That was Judy Evanson, dressed as an attendant. She apparently told your girl you'd been in an accident leaving the terminal, and you were calling for her. Schell was the one who made the call to distract you."

"I don't get it. How was the Evanson woman involved in this?"

"I don't know all the particulars, but she was Aaron Small's sister. She'd been adopted out right after she was born, and Aaron never saw her again. That is until after he came back from the war. He had always wanted to get her back. I think she's the only woman he ever cared about. He hired a statistical research company to trace her whereabouts. He somehow knew that the family who adopted the child was named Evanson."

"I'll be damned. So he did have some human feelings after all."

"I think that was the sum total of it though. He was a cold customer."

"So he found her. Then what happened? Did she just go with him unquestioning?" This whole thing was a surprise to me. I remembered the look on her face when I waited so long in that office to get a glance at whoever occupied the place. There was no way either of them wanted me to see his face."

"Apparently both her adoptive parents were deceased, and Aaron was the only family she had left. So she came to Chicago, and he set her up as his secretary."

"Do you think she knew what he was into?"

"I don't know if he told her, but I know she figured it out. She didn't have anything to do with the attempted murder of Chris Ellison, or Jerry Greenway's death. When she found out about Greenway, she cried. I think she really cared for the guy. But the strange thing was, the cop Rusty Ingalls was into her too. I guess she was q uite a player."

"Rusty Ingalls, who was he?"

"He was the other one who hassled you, and brought you to Aaron Small. The shorter one."

"What was the big guy's story?"

"He was just greedy, I guess. He was a little sadistic."

I replied, "Tell me about it." I couldn't help my sarcastic tone. "So what do you think will happen to the Evanson woman now?"

Chase thought for a second before answering, "She won't get off altogether, because she knew what was going on, and didn't report it. She will probably be charged as an accessory. She may have to serve some time."

"Okay, one more question and you can go back to your paperwork."

"Gee thanks." Chase smiled.

"What was the body count? Did they all die?"

"No. Small was dead, and Manny, along with one of the cops, the big one. His name was Delbert Grimes." He continued, "The smaller of the two policemen Ingalls survived, though he's in serious condition with a bullet lodged in his shoulder, and he'll face a tough inquiry, with probably a few years in prison."

"Delbert's parents must have had a hell of a sense of humor to name him that. Maybe that's why he turned out so tough. He probably had a lot of fights over the name."

"Could be." Chase answered politely.

Harry Shields came in just as Chase and I were finishing our conversation. He walked over to me and, shaking my hand, said, "I'm glad I ran into you Dunn. I wanted to tell you that, because of the police involvement with the mob, and a general housecleaning that's just beginning over there at the downtown precinct, you're off the hook on that assault charge. Considering that Manny was deep into the corruption, along with the two officers who were shot, they decided to drop all charges against you."

"That's a relief. It's too cold to stay in Chicago. I need to get back to a milder climate. My skin's not as thick as you guys."

Harry Shields laughed. "Yeah, we're tougher all over." Then he added, "Agent Chase and his lovely bride will be leaving too, but they'll be going back to a colder climate in the Pacific Northwest. Strangely they seem happy about it."

Later, as Rachel and I were driving out to the airport from the hotel, I saw a panhandler on the last corner of the downtown district. "I'm going to stop." I told Rachel.

"Oh no, not again." She answered with a frown that screwed up her beauty only slightly.

As I handed the man on the street corner ten dollars, I flashed her a toothy grin, and said, "Live with it."

The end of a novel
By
Frank A. Perdue

Be sure to read the last two installments of the Shadows series, Shadow of a Killer and Return from the Shadows.

Made in the USA
Charleston, SC
07 December 2016